*Right Trusty
and Well Beloved…*

Praise on Amazon for *Right Trusty and Well Beloved...* and *Grant Me the Carving of My Name* (the previous anthology inspired by King Richard III)

'An inspired idea.'

'A mixture of the serious and the light-hearted, this anthology of Ricardian short stories is a must read.'

'A great compilation ... I love the idea that it is raising money for Scoliosis UK as well. A highly entertaining read.'

'Great book and brilliantly written.'

'What an enjoyable, entertaining, and (at times) heart-rending collection of short stories.'

'An excellent and entertaining series of short stories and poems. Some are exciting, some amusing, some tragic and will make you cry.'

'With a little something for everyone, this anthology delivers. I found the mix of genres very clever. Curl up with this book and enjoy a journey that will yield a rainbow of emotion and adventure. Well done to all the authors who contributed!'

Right Trusty and Well Beloved...

An anthology of short fiction and poetry inspired by
King Richard III

With a foreword by
Philippa Langley MBE

Edited by
Alex Marchant

Sold in support of Scoliosis Association UK

Also available:

Grant Me the Carving of My Name

First published 2019 by Marchant Ventures

Copyright © 2019 the contributors

Editorial selection and introduction copyright © 2019 Alex Marchant

Further copies can be ordered from Alex at
AlexMarchant84@gmail.com

The right of the contributors to be identified as the authors of this work has been asserted in accordance with the Copyright, Design and Patents Act, 1988.

All rights reserved. No part of this publications may be reproduced, stored in or introduced to a retrieval system, or transmitted, in any form or by any means, electronic, mechanical, photocopying, recording or otherwise, without the prior permission of the copyright holder.

ISBN: 9781696761383

Cover illustration: © 2019 Frances Quinn

To the memory of

Josephine Tey

who brought so many of us to King Richard

Contents

Foreword by *Philippa Langley MBE* — ix
Acknowledgements — xi
Introduction — 13
This Life, This Death, This Life *Elizabeth Ottosson* — 17
Let Him Fly That Will *Kit Mareska* — 20
Richard the Third, by Thomas More *Susan Grant-Mackie* — 28
The Wife beside Doncaster *Wendy Johnson* — 33
York Freedom March *Kathryn Wharton* — 44
King Edward's Court, October 1468 *Brian Wainwright* — 46
If Only… *Alex Marchant* — 55
The Play's the Thing *Kit Mareska* — 60
Grief *Joanne R. Larner* — 74
The Silent Boy *Nicola Slade* — 77
Cerne Abbey, 1471 *Rebecca Batley* — 90
The Corners of my Mind *Richard Tearle* — 95
Becoming White Surrey *Máire Martello* — 103
The Lady of the White Boar *Jennifer C. Wilson* — 118

Richard Redux *Terri Beckett*	126
War of Words *Joanne R. Larner*	136
The Men and the Monument *Liz Orwin*	144
Eboracum *Kim Harding*	159

Foreword
Philippa Langley MBE

In November 2018, Alex Marchant published *Grant Me the Carving of My Name*, a collection of short stories inspired by Richard III in aid of Scoliosis Association UK (SAUK). The volume, comprising stories from a number of authors, has sold worldwide and raised awareness not only of 'good King Richard', but also of the condition from which he suffered, and that continues to affect many people today.

When it was revealed that the king had suffered from scoliosis, so much about the man was revealed with it. We now understand why those contemporaries who had met and described him did not mention anything unusual about his appearance. It was only following his death, when the scoliosis became known, that the Warwickshire priest and antiquarian John Rous described Richard as having one shoulder higher than the other (a clear sign of the condition). However, Rous did not know which shoulder was the higher and left a gap in his account so that it could be recorded later. In having this condition Richard joins a distinguished group of well-known names such as Elizabeth Taylor, Princess Eugenie, Kurt Cobain and John Lydon, together with many world champion and record-breaking athletes such as the powerlifter Lamar Gant, tennis player James Blake, once ranked number four in the world, Olympian swimmer Janet Evans, and of course the fastest man in the world, Usain Bolt.

Today numerous authors, artists, poets, sculptors and creatives of all kinds are inspired by Richard III, not only myself as a writer/producer. In this anthology you will read the work of some of them. One story, the intriguing 'War of Words' by Joanne Larner, suggests, with great skill and perception, that the pen has ever been mightier than the sword.

King Richard inspired great loyalty during his lifetime, and continues to inspire loyalty to this day. Much of this derives from the contemporary records from his lifetime and the loyal, brave, pious and just man these accounts reveal: a man who stands in stark contrast to the monster promulgated by Shakespeare and the Tudor writers.

The mystery surrounding the disappearance of the sons of King Edward IV is the final piece of the jigsaw of Richard's story and perhaps you can help solve it. *The Missing Princes Project*, launched in 2016, needs archivists and specialists in palaeography and Latin so that new archival material can be located and analysed. It is our belief that the truth is waiting to be found, in the same way that the king's grave was located, against the odds, in 2012. You can visit *TMPP* at: http://www.revealing richardiii.com/ langley.html.

Like the king's discovery, this landmark research project is already having an effect, with the sons of Edward IV no longer described as 'murdered' but correctly and factually as 'missing'.

I commend this anthology to you and the talented creatives whose work has inspired it.

Edinburgh
September 2019

Acknowledgements

We would like to thank all the contributors for generously donating their work to this anthology, and also everyone who entered the competition for submissions and donated directly to Scoliosis Association UK at that time. The standard of entries was very high and made selection of the final pieces included here extremely difficult.

We would particularly like to thank Frances Quinn for her fantastic image of King Richard and his loyal companions on Ambion Hill used on the cover. (Prints of a similar image are available to buy from Frances: see details below.)

Very special thanks are owed to Philippa Langley MBE for kindly providing a Foreword – and, of course, for her and her 'Looking for Richard' colleagues' painstaking and persistent work in finding King Richard's grave in the first place – which provided the catalyst for the stories and poems that are published in these pages.

The following has been previously published in a slightly different form and we would like to acknowledge permission to reproduce it here.

'The Silent Boy' was originally published in *The House at Ladywell* by Nicola Slade, published by Crooked Cat Books, 2017.

About the cover artist

Frances Quinn lives in Dublin, Ireland in a house filled with books, antlers and art supplies. A self-taught artist who occasionally dabbles in writing, her interest in Richard III dates back to the early 1980s when she read Josephine Tey's *The Daughter of Time*.

Examples of Frances' art can be found on the Internet at DeviantArt.com and on her Facebook page.

Website: https://www.deviantart.com/echdhu
Facebook: https://www.facebook.com/theArtofFrancesQuinn/

Introduction

'Right Trusty and Well Beloved…'
As many readers will know, this is the form of address that English (and British) monarchs have used to begin official letters for centuries, but it is perhaps now most associated in many people's minds (even before this anthology!) with King Richard III, the last of the Plantagenet kings – perhaps the last king of England who was part of the medieval system by which monarchs relied on personal ties for the success of their rule. These were usually personal ties of loyalty between king and nobility. Nowadays, though, for many of us, it perhaps denotes new ties – those of Ricardians to this long-maligned king.

And once again, in this book, Ricardians have come together to show their continued support for good King Richard. It's more than a year since I first had the idea of drawing together short stories inspired by the king into a collection aimed at raising awareness – both of him and of the painful spinal condition, scoliosis, that he was revealed to have had when his grave was rediscovered in 2012. A dozen writers contributed stories to that first anthology, *Grant Me the Carving of My Name*, and dozens more asked if they could submit stories and poems to any future collection. So it wasn't difficult to decide to edit a second book that would also raise money in support of Scoliosis Association UK (SAUK), the charity that offers advice and practical support to people today with the same condition (https://www.sauk.org.uk/).

These stories cover a range of genres and styles, and offer differing views on King Richard and his times. But all seek to portray the king in a more realistic light than the most famous depiction of him – William Shakespeare's remarkable, charismatic, witty, but largely inaccurate portrait of him in *The Tragedy of Richard III.* 'Realistic' at least in terms of character – if not, in fact, in terms of circumstances. King Richard could never, of course, have met the Bard of Avon, as he does in these pages. Nor, sadly, did he ever get the chance to decide on punishments to mete out for the treachery against him at the Battle of Bosworth...

Nor could Richard know of the blackening of his reputation that occurred in the decades and centuries after his death, through the writings, first, of Tudor-era historians with their agenda to glorify the usurper who took his crown, then of those who chose not to look beyond that so-called 'history' – beyond what has recently been described to me as 'the original fake news'. But I for one like to think that he would appreciate the efforts now being made across the globe (including in places he never even knew existed, such as the USA and New Zealand) to turn the tide of misinformation that led to the grotesque picture that many people still have of him. This 'war of words' (and images and songs) may yet lead 'the towers of Tudor lies' to come 'crashing down ... defeated by their own weapons', as Jo Larner says in her story in this collection.

The stories and poems featured in these pages are a small part of those efforts but, as they say, 'constant dripping of water wears away stone, not through force but through persistence', and Ricardians can be very persistent! We have to be, to counter five centuries of the 'traditional history' – although the first drips of resistance to that Tudor-era view began only a few years after the death of the last Tudor monarch, Elizabeth I, when James I's master of the revels Sir George Buck wrote his defence of Richard in 1619.

Persistence is very much something that Philippa Langley, who has kindly written our Foreword, knows all about. Without an abundance of it, she would never have been able to overcome the many obstacles in the way of her quest to find King Richard's grave, alongside her colleagues in the Looking for Richard Project (one of whom, Wendy Johnson, I'm delighted to say has again contributed a story in this anthology). And, perhaps, Philippa's continued persistence may lead to the resolution of one of the greatest mysteries in history: what happened to the sons of Edward IV, popularly known as the 'princes in the Tower'. Philippa's 'Missing Princes Project' continues to search for information to shed light on their fate. In her Foreword, Philippa shows how you can offer your help for the project.

If you enjoy the stories and poems in this book, please do check out the authors' details at the end of each piece. Maybe you'll enjoy their other works and you can, of course, show your support for them by 'liking' or following them at their websites or on social media (where shown).

This book is dedicated to the memory of Josephine Tey, one of our illustrious predecessors among 'warriors with words' rather than swords, whose remarkable novel *The Daughter of Time* led many of us to question the, until then, received history of good King Richard III.

Alex Marchant
October 2019

This Life, This Death, This Life

Elizabeth Ottosson

In the end you were so tired. You lay where you were thrown, your skin dissolving to bone, while above you kings and queens fought over lovers, descendants, God.

It was a long leaving, a life crumbling to its end. You lost young Edward and Anne; before them your brothers; after, still others. Rumours scattered among the populace like tabloid scandals, while you groped for allies who evaporated at your touch.

You were tired, angry, heartbroken at the betrayals and disappointments. So when death finally came you lay quiet – resting not in your northern home, but resting all the same.

*

For centuries you lie, while above you a kingdom collapses and is reborn. Your kindly God turns dour, but letters spread, no longer the voice of a privileged few. Buildings grow taller, clothes tighter and looser, tighter and shorter. Industries exhale smoke in a pall over cities grown up since your reign. The bones of the church above you are torn down but yours remain, silent in the resting earth.

Schoolboys run over your head, ghosts of Edward and his long-dead cousins. Too late for regret; the memory of what was done, or not done, has faded with the centuries.

*

After the long leaving, the reversal begins slowly. Your reputation, shredded by a century of Tudor propaganda, starts to revive. Scholars put forward evidence, to the scorn and dismissal of their contemporaries. Amateur sleuths pick up the trail, putting your life on trial.

Then comes the novel, a medium you never knew: authors exploring the zeniths and crises of your life in vertiginous detail, creating ripples, then waves of empathetic readers. A Fellowship is created, followed by a Society. A museum opens on your old home ground.

Your bones cannot move, but the dirt around them stirs, just a little.

*

Finally, a convergence of opportunity, money, momentum, will. Your bones are brought to light, scrutinized by technologies you would have viewed as magic.

A diagnosis is confirmed and a face emerges: kind, akin to the portrait of the time. A debate ensues: should you rest where you lay undisturbed all those years? In Westminster Abbey, near Anne? Up north, where your memory was kept alive long after it faded to cliché in the south?

Five hundred years is a strong claim. You remain in the city that grew up over your head, near the last battle of your hectic life.

*

'*...most piteously slain and murdered to the great heaviness of this city.*'

In thirty-two years you were soldier, son, father, brother, husband, protector (of the north, of the realm). Bound by loyalty in a reign riven by betrayal, you were the last English king to die in battle, and even your enemies – even Shakespeare – said you fought bravely. You lived more lives than most do in three times your age.

Rest now, Richard. Lay down your cares one final time. Mingle with your Anne, with Edward, with all the others you once loved.

Rest now, and let others carry you on.

Note: '*King Richard, late mercifully reigning over us, was most piteously slain and murdered to the great heaviness of this city*' *was recorded in the annals of the City of York after the Battle of Bosworth.*

About the author

Elizabeth Ottosson is a writer and translator whose stories have been published in various anthologies and shortlisted for awards on two continents. 'Grace', her very short story about Grace Darling, won the Segora International Vignette Competition, and Elizabeth is currently submitting a novel to agents. Her stories often focus on memory and connections, both lost and found.

As a teenager Elizabeth frequently dragged her family and friends to Middleham to hunt for signs of Richard III, so she is delighted to be part of this anthology.

Website: https://elizabethottosson.com/
Twitter: https://twitter.com/liza_belle

Let Him Fly That Will

Kit Mareska

Mid-August 1462

Westminster Palace is empty. Oh, my council still meets daily, priests still hold masses, I do not lack for servants eager to do the slightest task for me. But between the lords I sent north to besiege Alnwick Castle and the others that summer in their rural manors, there are fewer voices in the hall at dinner. Fewer hands at cards. Fewer friends with whom to hunt. And so when my lady mother writes, saying that she has a matter to discuss and wishes to pay me a visit, I answer that instead I shall come to her at Greenwich.

Mother has been busy adding white roses to Greenwich's gardens, their purity either lightening a rich carpet of greenery or lending a resting space for the eye amidst a tumult of other flowers' colours.

'The gardens are lovely, Mother. Greenwich shall never lack for Yorkist roses now.'

'None of your palaces should,' she says, although my compliment softens her expression. Only for an instant, however. Even before she speaks, I see that she is about to come to the reason for this audience.

'Edward, more than a year has passed since you assumed the throne. While I certainly understand that the running of a kingdom keeps you occupied, it does not stop time from passing.'

'Your beauty seems to disagree.'

Colour rises to her cheeks, but she waves an impatient hand.

'What I am saying, if you will spare me your courtier's tongue, is that your brothers have grown a year older without dedicated male guidance, and the lack is telling more by the day.'

She allows me to guide her to a bench beneath a willow tree, where her face looks no less pained for the rest.

I ask, 'Has something happened?'

'George does not like that you gave the honour of Richmond to Dickon.'

'I gave George several of Northumberland's manors.' Henry Percy, the Earl of Northumberland, was killed at Towton and I have yet to reverse his attainder or release his heir from the Tower.

'Yes, you did. But the castles that fall within the honour of Richmond are worth far more than those few Northumbrian manors. You know it well and so does George.'

'Because he's petty,' I mutter.

'Because he is heir to the throne! You went over his head to give one of the wealthiest honours in England to a nine-year-old boy and George understandably resents it. You may favour Dickon, but you must not *act* on those feelings so openly. It was a mistake, and I want you to rectify it.'

I tip my head back for a moment, looking at the willow leaves above, every possible shade of green from yellowish to a bluish silver. Our castle at Fotheringhay has a couple of willows like this growing alongside the River Nene. Edmund and I used to gather fat handfuls of branches and swing out on August days, dropping into the water below.

'Does George remember that I also made him Deputy of Ireland? He doesn't even have to do any work for that, just appoint his own deputy, sit back and claim the pay.'

'He remembers. He knows, as well, that you gave most of the Earl of Oxford's holdings to Dickon.'

The old Earl of Oxford rebelled against me privately rather than on a field of battle, but he is just as dead now as the Earl of Northumberland.

'Those are likely temporary. I'm still hoping to win over Oxford's son, given time. Dickon will have to surrender those properties when I do.'

'And he should surrender Richmond now. Before you find permanent places – *separate* places – for them to complete their educations.'

She rarely leans so hard, knowing her words weigh heavily enough on my scale as it is.

'I shall do as you ask, Mother. But I need a little time to decide where to send them and how to tell Dickon about Richmond. It won't be today. Or tomorrow. I'm moving the court to Windsor.'

I stand and offer her my arm.

She takes hold, saying, 'Very well: if not today, then soon. Promise me, Edward.'

It is not until we reach the palace and I see Dickon's blackened eye that I understand the reason for her leaning.

*

After a bountiful supper, I bend to kiss my mother's cheek in farewell.

'Wait a few days,' I say softly, 'then send Dickon to me at Windsor. If I'm going to deprive him of Richmond, I'll do it to his face.'

*

The bruise under Dickon's eye has faded to a blotted, ireful yellow by the time he arrives at Windsor. After I persuade him to have a second piece of bilberry pie at supper, I take him to see a young peregrine falcon I recently bought, who arrived just an hour before Dickon himself.

It's too soon to loose the peregrine. She hasn't settled from her journey and I want her to get used to me first. Therefore we merely walk, the falcon on my gloved left wrist, Dickon on her other side.

'So,' I ask, as we reach the edge of the deer park, 'are you ready to tell me yet who stained your eye?'

He wouldn't say at Greenwich, with George present, and I can see from the sudden hunch of his narrow shoulders that he still doesn't want to. Nor does the young Duke of Gloucester want to lie to his king.

'I'd rather not, Your Grace.'

'I can appreciate that. No man respects a tell-tale. Unless you tell me otherwise, I'll just continue in my belief that it was George.'

His mouth opens, a smear of bilberry like a fresh bruise at one corner.

'How'd you know?'

'There aren't many who'll take a swing at a royal duke, lad. It pretty much requires another royal duke.'

'He said he was sorry . . . after.'

After – when our lady mother found out and threatened to thrash him, no doubt.

'Did he? That's good to hear. Because I have to do something that I don't like and George very much shall. I have to take the honour of Richmond from you, Dickon, and give it to him.'

The young brow furrows over the dark blue eyes. He says nothing, just nods. I'm reminded that this same boy told my mother to send him into exile less than two years ago so that I would be unfettered in my fight for the crown. He is quick to accept what he does not want.

That doesn't make it right.

'I may have been wrong to give it to you, and I'm hoping the correction will restore the balance. I fully intend to find you other compensation, Dickon. I just don't know quite how, yet.'

We walk for several moments amidst the oaks without speaking, his jaw– our father's jaw – thrust further out than it was when we began. Gradually that jaw recedes and he glances at the peregrine.

'She *is* a beauty,' he says at last. 'Do you have a name for her?'

'Not yet. She should prove easy to train, though; peregrines generally are. I suspect she's sleepy enough now that you could try stroking her.' I halt and Dickon steps closer. 'Just her back. Stay away from that beak.'

He is careful, even reverent, this brother of mine, as his fingertips trail slowly down the grey feathers. I don't think I was ever so serious at that age. But then, I did not grow to manhood in the shadow of Wakefield.

'Dickon, you know that among the nobility, boys are usually sent to train for knighthood in the household of another noble.'

'Yes, Sire,' he says, withdrawing his hand from the bird.

'You also know why we couldn't do that for you earlier. Things are more settled now, though – as settled as they're likely to be for a while, at least, and Mother has asked me to find a place for you. Not because of anything you've done, or even because of anything George has done, but because it's just . . . *time.*'

'I understand, Your Grace.' His high voice sinks a bit and his hand strays to the assurance of the small knife at his belt.

I begin to walk again.

'What do you know of the north?'

'That it's cold . . . and vast and wild. That it's where you won at Towton. And it's where . . . where Edmund and Father were killed at Wakefield.'

Marvellous. Now he'll fear that he'll die in the north, like them. *Do better, Edward.*

'It is all those things. It's also quite beautiful in parts, with hills and rocky coasts and mighty castles. Our cousin Warwick's castle at Middleham is among the mightiest and so big they call it the Windsor of the north. That's where I want to send you.'

'George, too?'

'No, just you.' I can't think of what to do with George. I'm looking to build alliances, not enmities, and no one would thank me for foisting that suppurating little pustule on them.

'Is Middleham very far?'

'I'll not lie to you, lad – it is. Further than Ludlow, further even than the city of York.'

'How far from London – more than a hundred miles?'

'More than two hundred. But less than three.' His fingers aren't just resting on his knife hilt now, they're squeezing it, letting go, squeezing again. 'It's right on the edge of the dale lands. All sorts of valleys and woods to explore, and waterfalls . . .'

Mercy of God, why am I rambling on about features of the land like some windy old tutor? I need to put myself in Dickon's place. It isn't as though I never stood in those shoes, after all . . .

'I was seven when I was sent away to Ludlow Castle. Cried myself to sleep every night that whole first month. And it wasn't that Ludlow was horrible. It was that Mother and Father had moved to Ireland, so not only did I not know the place where I was, I *really* had no idea of where they were. Felt like I'd never see them again.

'But I did have Edmund. Even though he was younger than me, he got me through. Never told a soul about all my tears, either. Warwick has two daughters, Isabel and Anne. Isabel's a year older than you, somewhat quiet, but I can't imagine a girl more likely to soothe and dry tears. Anne . . .' I shake my head and smile. 'I don't know if Anne is a shoulder to cry on – she's four years younger than you, but I should think she'll lead you into all the right kinds of trouble.'

There's still no trace of a smile, but his hand has fallen from his knife. So I keep going.

'I grew to love Ludlow faster than I would have dreamed. And I think you'll grow to love the north –

which *is* part of England, no matter how close to Scotland it is. That's why I have to have control over it if our realm is to know peace. That's also why Warwick has been spending all his time there, because he knows it is a treasure both difficult to win and important to hold. But Warwick . . . well, as hard as he works, he can't be everywhere at once. I can't, either. That's why I need someone there whom I can truly trust and on whom I can depend. Warwick is older than me by almost fifteen years. Someday he won't be able to do everything he does now, and I shall need someone to help him, if not take his place altogether.'

The midnight eyes are on the ground; he's listening hard.

'You want me to go and find someone who could take Warwick's place.'

I stop, and he does, too. Then I reach out my birdless hand and raise my brother's beardless chin.

'Nay, Dickon – I want you to grow to *become* that man.'

He draws a deep and sudden breath, then a smile outshines the setting sun below his eye.

There are many things I do not tell him as we walk back to the lower ward. That I wish it were George and not him I am sending far away. That I do not entirely trust Warwick but cannot think of a better choice. I confine myself to saying that I shall miss him and hope he finds time, amidst all his adventures, to write to me. He promises to do so and I believe him.

We reach the mews. As I duck my head to enter the small building full of perches, the groom there asks if I have any special instructions for the new bird.

'Perhaps you'd better ask the Duke of Gloucester,' I say, even though this was not my plan when we began our walk. 'She's his falcon now.'

After several minutes of grinning and thanks, we step back into the full sunshine.

'Don't let George learn of her, though,' I warn. 'I'm of no mood to buy him one.'

'Edward . . .'

I stop. It is the first time my brother has used my name all day.

'I just wanted you to know . . . It was George who got me through the exile in Burgundy. Especially the days on the ship.'

'Now *that* truly *is* good to hear. Thank you, Dickon.'

I keep him with me at Windsor all through September. When October comes, we fly the peregrine on Dickon's tenth birthday. He names her Richmond.

Once Dickon departs for Middleham, I return to Westminster and name him Admiral of England, Aquitaine and Ireland. Lady mother or not, I am finished pretending that I have no preference between my brothers.

About the author

Kit Mareska is American, at least in this lifetime. Having majored in creative writing and minored in history at Miami University in Ohio, married her best friend and given birth to two wonderful daughters, she is now living in Pennsylvania and working full-time on a series of novels that centres on the friendship between King Edward IV and his chamberlain, William Lord Hastings.

Kit is profoundly thrilled to have two stories in this anthology, her first-ever publication. 'Let Him Fly That Will' is adapted from one of her novels-in-progress, while, as if writing kings wasn't already daunting enough, 'The Play's the Thing' was written specifically for this collection.

Website: https://www.kitmareska.com/
Facebook: https://www.facebook.com/KitMareska

Richard the Third, by Thomas More

Susan Grant-Mackie

Thomas More had writer's block. He also had a headache. And writer's cramp.

He stood up from his desk and walked to the window. His own reflection was fractured by the solder that pieced together the panes of glass; the candles in his study threw his own ghost back at him against the night.

And that, he realized with sudden clarity, was his problem. He'd set out to write the history of King Richard the Third, tyrant and child-killer, killed in battle in 1485. Thomas, now forty years old, had been a young child during those tumultuous events, so he'd turned to others to learn about Richard. But the more people talked about him, the more elusive Richard became.

Master More, Undersheriff of London, was initially happy to begin shovelling through Richard's bones. Richard deserved to have his bones shovelled through. Thomas had grown up listening to his elders and betters agreeing that Richard had been cast into hell and suffered in torment. Because he was deformed in body and mind and killed children. Worse, he went into battle against King Henry which was treason, because Henry was king the day before the battle. That was the law.

What a great project to dig into and get on record! Easy.

But Thomas now sighed and hugged his fur cloak tighter around himself, because the room had become cold and he was suddenly afraid. Not of ghosts but of the living. His own reflection told him that in trying to grasp Richard, he was only collecting the rattling, dry bones of the guilty and the liars. Not the bones of Richard at all. They were gone, silent, resting. Untouchable forever.

Thomas had only got as far as Richard's birth and early years when he first thought, 'You must be jesting!' He actually laughed. Oh yes, he had been told, Richard's birth had been a nightmare and he was born with teeth and a hunched back and a withered arm. He probably had his crutches in tow. That's how evil he was. He was an ugly child, and how evil is that?

Unless the laws of nature had suddenly changed just for baby Richard, all this was nonsense. And Thomas said so.

'Dear Reader, this is what they told me. Believe it if you want, but I don't.'

Thomas was also told that Richard was responsible for the slaughter of many; at least Henry, the sixth of that name, and Richard's own brother, George, the Duke of Clarence. Oh, they told Thomas, yes, Richard complained about his brother's death, but not loud enough. What was 'loud enough'? Thomas ponders. Yes, and Richard probably killed Henry, the sixth of that name, *personally*! And Thomas sighs… ye gods.

The idiot who told him this lurid tale was replaced by another idiot who wanted Thomas, and his readers, to believe that Richard had murdered his young nephews. Thomas noted down the story of dark deeds in the middle of the night, but then began to doubt.

Nobody knew where the two boys had gone. Certainly not in Richard's lifetime – nor now. Yet, the fool who sat before him had told a horror story that could only have lurched out of an unhinged mind. Or a talented one. Richard plots the boys' murder while in the privy. How evil and horrible is that, discussing murdering children while you're sitting on the 'throne'? It's all dark and leery and hunch-backy slithery.

Then Richard and a random page leave the privy and stumble upon two likely hit men in bed together. The hit men – presumably still in bed and alarmed by the rude interruption – are sounded out about killing the young lads. 'Yes, sure thing, we'll kill your nephews. What a great idea! *When will this lunatic go away and leave us alone?*'

And the boys are smothered in their beds. Then their graves are dug through stone in the Tower of London. Then someone gets a guilty conscience and has the boys' bodies dug up and moved somewhere else.

What a bloody farce! All the hammering and digging involved in making graves within the Tower; bodies buried then unburied; boys thrashing for their lives. And yet, not one of the hundreds of people who call the Tower of London home, or work there by day, heard or saw anything? At all?

Thomas has been told, on excellent authority – from excellent idiots – that the boys' bodies were carried around the place by the hit men, and then unburied, then carried around somewhere else by someone else. Without being found out. Without once coming across one of the hundreds of people who live in the place? And if they did run into someone with two bodies over their shoulders, how did they explain that? A sack of coal? Provisions for the kitchens? Did a memo go out explaining 'nothing to see here'? Or maybe the lions from the menagerie had escaped and run amok and needed to be killed and buried in secret at the foot of some stairs...

And by the time the boys' bodies were dug up again at the order of the conscience-stricken guy, there'd have been an awful stench. And more hammering and clattering and moving of stones. But not a word, not one single ribbon of gossip from the Tower to follow. Never.

Thomas smelt the smell of lies. These stories were ridiculous. And he walked to his desk and jotted down, 'If you believe all this... you need your head examining.'

He scribbled this out, thought a bit, then wrote: 'If you are going to tell lies, you might as well make them very big lies.'

He was angry. How stupid did these liars think he was? He swore and threw his pen down. Ink bled everywhere.

His faith in the damn project had drained away. About the time he got to the description – from some other idiot – of Richard behaving like an eye-rolling, drooling lunatic because he was supposed to have developed a conscience – either that or he'd hit the red wine a bit hard. After thirty-two years of looking ugly with withered arms and a hunchback, and quite happily murdering everyone in his family. After all that time, the conscience pays an overnight visit and Richard loses his mind.

Cobblers he did.

In the middle of some excruciatingly boring and lengthy conversation between important people just before the Battle of Bosworth Field, Thomas realized he wasn't going anywhere with this.

Stuff the battle. We all know how it ends. Liars win.

But, more importantly, stuff hanging all this rubbish on Richard's shoulders. Maybe the king, Henry, the eighth of that name, wanted it, but Thomas More wasn't going to be the one to do it.

He swore again, snatched up the parchments, rolled them up and tossed them deep into the bowels of the elaborate oak cabinet in which he kept his private papers. The angels carved on its belly smiled at him ... Maybe the smiling angels were just a trick of the firelight, but that is where Thomas left the liars. With the angels and God. Let them deal with it all.

Treachery, deceit and ruthless deeds by the living were being hung on the shoulders of one man. Because he was dead. He had lost the battle, so he could take it. He had no choice.

Thomas More had a choice, though.

His heart missed a beat as sparks spat into the room and a pyre of burned-out logs in the fireplace crashed into a cauldron of embers. He looked around, suddenly terrified; someone might have heard his thoughts and gone straight to the king. Who was possibly the son of a usurp...

But no one else was there. In this small room with its cackling fire, candlelit shadows and hidden liars.

It was treason to even think bad thoughts about the king. But Thomas and Richard were not going to tell anyone.

Yet...

About the author

Susan Grant-Mackie lives in Wellington, New Zealand. She is editor of two magazines, and when not in the office, enjoys reading and writing about history, with a particular focus on individuals who influenced and surrounded Richard III and Henry VIII. Her interest in Richard III was sparked by Josephine Tey's *The Daughter of Time*. She says it may also owe something to her many Yorkshire ancestors.

The Wife beside Doncaster

Wendy Johnson

If only she had eaten the last piece of wheaten bread, hard and dry though it was. If only she had swigged the last stale dregs of barley beer. Perhaps, if she had, the road ahead would not quiver and blur, rise up to meet her in fitful waves. Perhaps she would not have to pause, wipe her face with the edge of her kerchief and search for the strength to go on.

But she could not have allowed herself all that remained of their paltry meal. Not while Adam gazed up at her, eyes like shiny black pebbles in their hollow sockets. Not while Mary whined, tiny hands making tiny fists as her belly groaned and griped. What mother would? What father?

'I will not have you resort to beggary!' Thomas had been determined, heaving himself up and gripping the edge of the table for support. 'My foot is near mended. And when it is, Master Berney says he will have me back—'

'Master Berney!' She had snatched her skirts from his grasp and hoisted Mary on to her hip in an attempt to comfort her. 'There'll be nowt from his coffers 'til you can shift a cornsack again. And in the meantime, we must eat, Tom!'

'A sennight, is all.'

'You said that last week. We cannot last. You have been without work for more than a month.'

His face had crumpled at that, and she had made for the door, unwilling to witness the hurt she had caused him. 'I'll take the childer with me, they may afford us some charity.'

'Margery, please! You know Father Gifford has promised us some relief —'

'But it is not enough.' Taking Adam's hand, she fumbled for the latch. 'And, besides, is that not also begging, Tom?'

'No, Margery! For shame!'

Turning her back on the lumbering figure, she had fled the cottage.

If begging is what is required, then begging is what she will do.

She understands. She feels for Tom: a proud man, a kind man, happy to dole out charity when times are good, but reluctant to accept it himself. She knows how much it has aggrieved him to accept Father Gifford's offer, how much the image of his wife begging by the roadside is as abhorrent to him as lifting his hand against her. And he has never done that, no matter how desperate they have become.

But she cannot allow his pride to ruin them. She must act. And there is only one way.

'Where to, Ma?' Adam trudges by her side, stoical, sedate. He could be following her to the town ditch, to the edge of the earth, or to the very jaws of Hell, for all he knows.

'To Friar's Bridge.'

'What for, Ma?' The boy's eyes are fixed on the ground, the energy required to lift his head better spent on walking.

'For charity.'

It was Auld Katheryn's idea. She knows a goodwife, she says, who knows another, whose husband has heard good things of him. Fair. Just. Willing to listen. Auld Katheryn says she saw him once, when he was but a youth and housed with his mighty cousin. If he learned his cousin's ways, Auld Katheryn says, then he'll be liberal with his alms.

Liberal. She hopes so. A hope, however femmer, however slight, is better than no hope at all, and she has made up her mind to take Auld Katheryn's word – to unfurl it like a ribbon and follow its trail up Frenchgate, to Friar's Bridge. If, when she gets there, she finds the ribbon is frayed and tattered, worn with disappointment and spattered with stains of her own gullibility, then she will wind it up and stuff it into her bodice to remind herself that she did at least try, and that whatever befalls them will not be from lack of striving.

It is nigh on noon. From the town she hears the bells of Saint George's and Saint Mary Magdalene's: flat clangs upon the still air. Her gown is tight, and sticky under her arms, her kerchief clinging to her neck with sweat. Trussed like a fowl, she feels exhausted. The road ahead begins to blur, sends her lurching. She reaches out, grips Adam's bony little shoulder.

'Let us stop. Just for a moment.' Pausing, she wipes her face, takes a deep breath. She longs to sit down, but dare not yield: if she does, she may not find the will to rise again. And she must. Whatever happens, she must not return home empty handed.

'Are you sick, Ma?'

'No.'

Mary's cry becomes a mewling whine and she shifts the child from one hip to the other, the wriggling body a dead weight.

'Ma?'

'Come, Adam. We must go on.'

Cottages, hovels, are thinning out as she struggles towards the Greyfriars. She should not feel this weary; they have come but a short way. A short way, perhaps, for a rider, or a strapping youth, or a flitting girl fresh from her mother's kitchen with the scent of new-baked bread clinging to her kirtle. But it is a long way for a woman with child; a half starving woman, who bears another in her arms, and who is followed so doggedly, so trustingly, by her wraith-like son. A very long way.

She thinks briefly of Tom. Confined to their pallet he can do nothing, except wait, and then berate her upon her return. *What are our lives,* he will say, *compared to his? Do the wealthy really know, when they dole out the remnants of their feast, how it is for those with the open palms and the empty bellies? They do it for Christian charity, in order to see them into Heaven. Well, if that's the way to Paradise, then it must be easy for the rich to glide through the gates, to wriggle their way out of Purgatory with records of their good deeds puffing out their purses.*

However she returns, with alms or without, she feels sure that Tom will be angry. The anger of a man who, in his own eyes, has failed his growing family. A man who wallows in the guilt of a thing not of his own making, but who will allow none other to remove that guilt from him – for it is his, and he must own it – must recompense his family in his own way, and with his own hands, or else he will have failed them twice over.

Pride, she tells herself again, has no place. Pride is for the vain and for the foolish, and her own hands are open for alms even if those of her husband are not.

She catches sight of the bridge and sends up a prayer. Just a few more yards, just a few more steps: one and another, then another. It is her intention to wait here, where the cavalcade will slow in order to navigate the narrow way. And it is her intention to be noticed.

'Are we stopping, Ma?'

She nods, too tired to reply. Sinking down, she allows herself the luxury of the hard ground, the parched grass. Mary snuggles into her, weary from her tears, while Adam finds a dry stick and seeks to amuse himself by making lines in the dust. The child inside her moves and she wonders what in God's name she will have to offer it. If it survives the birth. If she does.

Unfastening the strings of her apron, she places the linen over Mary's head, to shield her matted curls from the sun. The child squeals at first, but she holds her close, whispering comfort she does not feel, clinging to the hope that Auld Katheryn is right. That he is fair: that he is just.

That God will move him, even if the sight of her wretched family does not.

Shading her eyes, she glances back the way they have come, sees figures shambling towards them in the heat. It seems others have had the same idea. Catch him as he comes in, before he reaches the marketplace, before his entourage is surrounded – by petitioners, by aldermen, by well-wishers, by whores. Some are simply curious, she can see that: goodwives in starched kerchiefs, men in their finest worsted. But others are clutching begging bowls, removing caps from their heads in anticipation of a tossed penny or two. She considers moving, walking further, so she will be completely alone and he will not fail to notice her. But the unseasonal heat is brutal and she is exhausted. This is her patch now and they shall stay here. All beggars have patches, places that they call their own. Let this be hers.

'Ma?'

Adam's voice, his eager pummelling fingers. She jerks upright, struggles to focus. She must have slept, but it cannot have been for long. Has she missed him? After all this effort. *Please God, no.*

'There are noises. Riders coming.' Adam's face is rigid, 'Is it safe here, Ma?'

She reaches out, flattens his hair, smooths his jerkin. 'On your feet.'

Will he care? Will he *really* care whether a child whose father toils in a humble mill is fit to be presented? Whether the child, or the one who toils, or their womenfolk, survive a day past Michaelmas?

She hauls herself up. Lifting the apron from Mary's head, she fastens it once more around her waxing belly, then takes the child in her arms.

'Adam. We will see a man, and when I tell you, you must bow your head. As you do when your father speaks to you. Do you understand?'

'Yes, Ma.'

She nods her approval, heart pumping.

In the distance, the tramping of hooves, the jingling of harness, visible clouds of rising dust.

'He is getting closer,' Adam says. 'The man.'

A legion of thoughts race through her head, as her breast tightens, her belly stirs. A brief, fleeting moment: that is all that will be allowed her.

Dust. Tramping. Jingling.

The gaggle of riders forms itself into distinct outlines; into men, into liveried men. Slowing its pace, the phalanx narrows, moves fluidly as it negotiates the bridge. The matter of a moment. Just a moment. And it is almost upon her.

Banners; bright, but limp in the still air. Scarlet and blue, leopards and lilies. A man: surrounded by other men, yet distinctive. Crimson silk, black bonnet. Pale face, fine, almost delicate, framed by heavy, curling brown hair. She sees how his companions defer to him, how they place themselves around him, sees the graceful movements of his hands as he speaks, how the others nod, smile at something he says, how one laughs aloud.

From the tail of her eye, figures looming, seeping like ink. Petitioners like herself, moving in. She must be the first to catch his eye, the first to throw herself before him. Now. She must speak now.

With Mary struggling, whining at her hip, she lunges forward.

'May God save Your Grace!'

His eyes are suddenly upon her: bright, sharp, curious. Velvet gloves with gilt thread, gently easing his mount to a halt. A word to his companions: commands are bellowed, horses reined in. The cavalcade halts.

But the cry has taken all her strength. Trembling, unsteady, she sinks to the ground.

'Ma?' Adam lays a hand on her shoulder.

'Ratcliffe!' An order: delivered like the crack of a whip.

A man dismounts. As finely dressed as his master, he is lithe, swift, has her on her feet in a moment.

The king draws his mount closer, leans down from the saddle, the collar that graces his shoulders glinting in the sunlight, its pendant jewel bobbing.

'Mistress.' The voice is low and strangely pleasant. 'You are in need of succour. Ask of me that I may help you.'

She closes her eyes, steadies her breathing. Recovering herself, she peers up at him. The slender face is delicate, yes, but steely, with a strong jaw. And the eyes miss nothing. Slate grey and intuitive, they take in all that is to be seen of her: her grubbiness, her weariness, her desperation.

'You *are* in need of my help,' he says. 'That I can see.'

Now that the moment has come, she is afraid. Afraid she may ruin the only chance she and her family have of survival.

'Highness. My family…we…' Coherence escapes her, like flour through her fingers.

'Yes?'

'My —'

'Me Pa, Sir.' Adam bows, steps forward, skinny little arms tight across his chest. 'Me Pa has a broken foot. Has to lie abed. We're hungry, and me sister cries all t'time.'

The grey eyes flick towards the boy, soften. A finger beckons.

'Come. Tell me.'

Wary of so large a horse, Adam hesitates before inching closer, starts as the great beast whinnies and shakes its head in a shower of spittle. The velvet gloves slide gently, lovingly, over the creature's glimmering hide.

'She will not harm you, boy. Come closer. And you, Mistress, if you please. I would hear of your difficulties.'

The pungent, earthy smell of his mount, the leather of its polished saddle, the waft of cinnamon and clove that rises with every movement of his sleeve.

Assailed by scents and colours, the beauty of his clothing, the intricacy of his jewels, of tassels, of gilded buckles, she feels unreal. She cannot be here. Not in this place, not in this moment: a breath away from God's anointed.

'Your husband?' He tries to make it easier for her, inclines his head, draws his narrow lips into a smile: a smile that serves to light up his face.

'Yes. My husband. Tom…Thomas Appleby. Works at Master Berney's mill. An accident. His toes crushed, broken. Not all, Highness, but…'

'But enough that he cannot walk. That he cannot *work*.'

A great, tight lump rises and wedges itself in her breast: the weeping she has withheld for many weeks, that she has constrained, forced back into the very depths of her being, fearful that, once released, its tidal wave would drown her.

'Perhaps—'

'He has not worked since before Lammastide. Our supplies are low, he is weak, we are all weak…' She has not addressed him with respect, has interrupted him in a way a subject should never interrupt a king, but she sees no creasing of his brows, no indignation, merely the deepening of concern.

'Any more children at home?'

She presses her daughter to her breast. 'No, Your Grace. Just Adam and Mary here. And another, yet to be born.'

He returns his attention to Adam, the look intent, the interest genuine.

'What age are you, boy?'

Adam shoots her a glance, 'Ma…?'

'He has just seen eight summers, Highness.'

'Eight summers.' The king compresses his lips, a distracted gesture, as if other things, more pressing, are tugging at his thoughts. Around him, his retinue is restless; horses snorting, bridles tinkling. He ignores them, lowers his gaze, makes a study of his linen cuffs. Discovering a loose thread, he takes it between his fingers.

'A family should not be cast asunder through want, or the vagaries of circumstance. A boy should not lose his father, nor a father his son.'

His head jerks up. 'A purse, if you please!'

Taut as a bowstring, she waits as the order is passed down the line. A clerk dismounts. Approaching the king, he proffers up a red leather purse. The king takes it, loosens its ties. Pouring a shower of silver into his gloved palm, he calculates.

'Three shillings and fourpence. Will this make it right?'

It is then that it bursts from her: the burden that has weighed her down like a millstone, that has crushed and strangled her, waking and sleeping, each and every day for the past month; that has borne her down into black depths, suffocating her until she feared she would perish from its weight.

Racked by sobs, she nods, as he presses the purse into her outstretched hand and closes her fingers around it.

Impulse compels her to reach out: to touch the toe of his boot, to bow her head and brush her lips across the dust-encrusted leather.

'May Jesu bless and keep Your Grace. How can we ever thank you?'

The face that looks down into hers is surprisingly tender.

'Every subject in my realm is entitled to charity, to justice. If I have helped you and your family, then I am glad, for that is my intention.'

Inclining his head, he settles back into his saddle and with a flick of the reins, nudges his mount forward. The cavalcade moves off: a rippling ribbon of colour.

She watches it go, watches others stumbling after it, calling out. She sees how he pauses, raising his hand in salute, how he is eaten up by the growing crowd.

Bread, salt-fish, bacon, cheese. They will eat well tonight, and every night, until Thomas is well.

Giving Mary a squeeze, she plants a kiss on the little girl's cheek.

Adam gazes up at her.

'That man,' he says, 'is he the king?'

She nods, joy and relief coursing through her, settling the fear in her heart, the child in her womb.

'Yes, my love,' she says. 'Yes. He is the king.'

'Warrant to Thauditors of Middelham to allow Geoffrey Fraunke, Receiver of the same, in his accomptes the summe of ... iijs iiijd to a wiff besides Doncastre by the kings commaundement.'
British Library Harleian Manuscript 433 [folio 118]

'He contents the people wherever he goes better than ever did any prince; for many a poor man that hath suffered wrong many days hath been relieved and helped by him and his commands in his progress ... On my troth, I liked never the conditions of any prince so well as his. God hath sent him to us for the welfare of us all.'
Thomas Langton, Bishop of St David's to the Prior of Christ Church, Canterbury, September 1483

About the author

Wendy Johnson has a passion for medieval history and, having been fascinated by the Wars of the Roses since childhood, she has been a member of the Richard III Society for more than thirty years. Her short stories and poems are a regular feature of the *Court Journal*, the publication of the Society's Scottish branch, and she was a finalist in the *Woman and Home* Short Story Competition in 2008, with a story set in fourteenth-century York.

Along with her husband, Dr David Johnson, Wendy was a founding member of Philippa Langley's *Looking For Richard Project*, which successfully located the lost grave of King Richard in 2012, and is a co-author of *Finding Richard III: The Official Account.* Wendy's other historical interests include the Angevin kings of England and the English Civil Wars of the seventeenth century. She is currently researching and writing a historical novel, set during the Wars of the Roses, which is intended to form part of a trilogy. Wendy lives in York, Richard III's favourite city.

Website: http://revealingrichardiii.com/index.html
Amazon: https://www.amazon.co.uk/Finding-Richard-III-Official-Account/dp/0957684029

York Freedom March

Kathryn Wharton

(BBC, 4 February 2013: *The skeleton remains found in a car park in Leicester 'are beyond reasonable doubt' the remains of King Richard III*)

Soldiers stand at the cenotaph ready to parade where old pals
march their names in stone. Ghosts hear an echo: *A horse. A
horse.*
A rose is a rose; but this white rose is blood soaked.
Forward march.

Drums roll, a bugle calls, spectators aim their camera phones
like snipers on the pavements.
Feet thump from left-to-right, arms synchronize, ranks take
commands
in baritone, but every Tommy shares his shilling.

Mark time, the captain bellows. Ghosts hear a battle cry,
feet grind their teeth in gravel:
Soldiers, raise your arms for York, all join a roar:
The key. The key.

Ghosts hear the metal rattle. Bones crack beneath the stone.
King Richard re-emerges, to take the freedom
of Old England's capital city:
Soldiers, raise your swords for Jorvik.

About the author

Kathryn Wharton is from Baildon, West Yorkshire, and 'York Freedom March' formed part of her MA in Creative Writing at Leeds Trinity University, completed in 2018.

Kathryn's previously published poetry includes: 'Song of Creation', in *Mythologies: A Space for Words* (Indigo Dreams Publishing, 2018); 'Yesterfear', in *Portmanteau* (Indigo Dreams Publishing, 2017); and 'I Am', in *Mslexia*, no. 74 (June–August 2017). Kathryn was also runner-up, with 'Poppies', in the British Army's competition 'Writing Armistice' (2018) and her 'Cap Badge' was also selected for the *Pendle War Poetry* anthology (2018).

Kathryn is currently preparing her first collection of poems for publication in 2020 by Runcible Spoon (www.runciblespoon.co.uk).

King Edward's Court, October 1468

Brian Wainwright

'If I were your husband, my lady, I should not be so discourteous as to neglect you for the sake of a game of cards.'

Elizabeth Mowbray, Duchess of Norfolk, had been unaware of Hastings's presence at her side; it was almost as if he had emerged from the wall instead of the shadows, the background noise of music and conversation cloaking his approach. She hesitated for a moment, then relaxed as she realised that there was nothing in her interrupted talk with Anne Montgomery that could be misrepresented. It did not matter how much or how little the Chamberlain had overheard.

'I am sure that is quite true, my lord. If I were your wife, you'd be neglecting me for one of your whores.'

In the face of so confident a reply William Hastings smiled; made an elaborate bow. 'I regret, my Lady Duchess, that you have so low an opinion of me. Indeed, of yourself, if you believe that I could be so easily distracted from such perfection.'

'I believe you have me mistaken, sir, for one who is impressed by empty flattery.'

He stood next to her, entirely at his ease, using his chamberlain's staff as a convenient leaning post. 'At one time or another, we have all been deceived by such words,' he said. 'The great question at court is ever the same. Whom may we trust? The answer, too, is ever the same - no one. We all pursue our own interests, our own advantage. Each of us wears a mask to hide our true intent, even the King; the King, perhaps, above all.'

Elizabeth did not answer, uncertain as to where the conversation was leading. Hastings was equally still and silent for a few minutes. Threateningly so, she thought. He smiled and nodded as acquaintances went by them, but that was all.

'However,' he went on, his voice as casual and as artificial as his pose, 'there's no deceit in declaring your beauty. It's visible to all, and I well remember that your sister was no less striking to the eye. It seems but yesterday that she came before the King in her widow's gown, to plead for the restoration of her lands.' He paused, and sighed. 'Lady Butler. What man could have resisted her? Not the King, that's sure. Did she ever speak to you of him?'

'Would there be cause for her to do so, Lord Hastings?' Her faint eyebrows lifted as she fought to conceal her discomfort, to appear merely puzzled.

'It may be that she had; for after that day she and the King were close for a time. Very close.' He laughed, at least half to himself. 'What woman could possibly hold her tongue about such a matter? That kind of intimate secret is always shared; if not with a friend, then perhaps with a sister. You see, my dear Duchess, I know something of ladies and their nature. It has been my lifelong study.'

'You might have been better employed, my lord, in studying ways to speak in plain words. If you are implying that my sister so far forgot herself as to become the King's mistress, then I say to your face that you lie in your teeth. She was a very pious woman and would never have thought of sharing a bed with any man but her husband. I will not permit you, or any other, to insult her memory and my family's honour.'

Elizabeth's anger was partly for effect, partly a disguise for her concerns. She turned abruptly and removed herself from Hastings's company as quickly as was possible without losing her dignity. The sea of courtiers parted before her, in deference to her rank and the fierceness of her expression, but she had not the least idea where her feet were taking her.

'That odious wretch dares to insult you,' Anne Montgomery hissed. 'My lady, you must tell the Duke of this; do not allow it to pass unchallenged.'

Elizabeth eased her pace a little. 'I'm told we may judge a man by his friends. Lord Hastings is the King's friend. Remember that, Nan, and be careful what you say of him. We are surrounded by tale-bearers.'

'I don't understand. What are you supposed to have done, that they treat you with such contempt?'

'They think I have made a pact with my Beaufort cousins, to put King Harry of Lancaster back on his throne.' Elizabeth covered her careful simplification with a glowing smile. 'I suppose I ought to be flattered, that they think me capable of such a feat. I must be a far greater lady than ever I imagined.'

'At least King Harry is a holy man; not a tyrant and murderer. I wish he *were* still ruling over us. My husband would still be alive; so would many other good men Edward of York has butchered.'

'Harry of Lancaster is in the Tower; we shall both join him there, if you do not take more care of your words.' Elizabeth cast around her, looking for eavesdroppers. In the semi-darkness of the room it was impossible to be absolutely sure. They were in an antechamber of the hall, a place where many had gathered to pass their time with friends. Someone was strumming at a lute, and there was a fair amount of raucous laughter, but no one seemed to be reacting to what her companion had said.

Elizabeth hesitated, wondering what she should do with herself. She was out of place here, where the company was almost exclusively male and unknown to her; on the other hand, she was still angry with her husband and in no haste to return to him. By now he would be deeply involved in his game of cards with Clarence and their cronies, risking absurd sums of money and gulping down wine by the pint. There was little entertainment in watching him make a fool of himself. She might attach herself to the Queen, of course, but the Queen was surrounded by an intimate circle, dominated by sisters and cousins, that did not go out of its way to welcome an outsider. It was an unattractive option, especially as it would involve retracing her steps and risking another interception by Lord Hastings.

Elizabeth moved on at a gentler pace, concealing her confusion behind an expression of trained composure, but still uncertain as to her destination. She passed through the arch leading into the adjacent dancing chamber. Here, on a vast floor tiled in red and cream chequers, a score of couples were engaged in a lively estampie dance to a jaunty tune provided by a gallery of royal musicians. The music caressed her ears and forced an unwilling sigh of pleasure from her lips. Dancing had been all her joy at the Burgundian court; such pleasures were rare at Framlingham.

She turned towards the nearest of the window recesses, looking for room to accommodate herself on one of the seats built into the curve of it. There were, however, occupants already in place. A slight, serious-looking young woman of about her own age dressed in a furred, green gown and, seated next to her, a boy of about fourteen, with a broad, smiling face and yellow hair. They rose to their feet at once, and the little woman made a formal curtsey.

'Cousin Norfolk!' she said, rising from it with every sign of delight. 'This is good fortune – I've been hoping that I might speak to you.'

Elizabeth somehow converted an impulse to walk away into a gracious gesture of consent. She settled down on the cushions and the others grouped themselves around her. Her cousinship with Lady Margaret Beaufort, the Countess of Richmond, could not be denied, but it was not a tie she was apt to emphasize. As for the boy, he was cousin to them both. Harry Stafford, Duke of Buckingham, husband of the Queen's sister, Katherine, and nephew of Margaret's present husband, Sir Henry Stafford. They were both, like her, born into great Lancastrian families; both doubtless mistrusted and watched by Edward's spies. In her present circumstances they made particularly uncomfortable company.

Lady Margaret had a great deal to say, but there was little Elizabeth thought to be of any great significance. She relaxed, and allowed the centre of her attention to shift to the dancers.

'I hear Paston is to marry the Haute girl,' Margaret said, with a sudden change of tone that startled Elizabeth. The couple in question were passing by them in the dance, their hopping steps and leaps perfect but their faces set in expressions that seemed designed to mask their enjoyment. 'I wonder whether that will cause trouble between your lord and the Queen. I don't suppose Norfolk intends to drop his claim to Caister?'

It seemed a casual question, but Elizabeth knew that it was not. That her cousin was prying for information.

'I don't think Paston's got much of a bargain there,' said young Buckingham, with a bright smile that temporarily dazzled Elizabeth. He laughed. 'Of course, the Queen is not noted for her generosity, as I have good cause to know. All she cares about is foisting her kindred off onto their betters. If I were you, Duchess, I'd take good care of Norfolk. If any ill befalls him you may find yourself in the same straits as his grandmother, married off to another Woodville.'

'Many have been happy to wed their sons and daughters into the Queen's family,' Margaret observed. Her voice was quiet and level, though her keen, bird-like eyes glanced around to be sure that no one else was within hearing distance. 'Not everyone, Nephew, is as proud of his ancient blood as you are. Some are all too happy to trim to the times if it will gain them a word in the King's ear.'

'Paston's barely a gentleman,' Buckingham answered. He stifled a yawn with his hand and leaned back against the cushions. 'Certainly the first knight in his family; his grandfather was a jumped-up lawyer. I still say he hasn't got much of a bargain. I doubt there'll be much of a dowry changing hands, and the girl must be the first lady I've ever seen with a waiting-woman better-looking than herself.'

The waiting-woman in question was dancing with Richard of Gloucester. Elizabeth remembered her face from the archery match earlier in the day, but did not know her name. She thought it an incongruous pairing until the progression of the couples enabled her to see the light in Gloucester's eyes. He was joyful, and it transformed his face. She had not thought him half as handsome as his brothers, until that moment.

'Another of the Queen's dirt-poor cousins,' Buckingham went on. He seemed more than faintly amused, his expression full of boyish spite. 'This one must have been instructed to get her hooks into Dickon. Though I doubt there's marriage in mind for those two. Not even Bess Woodville would be as bold as that.'

Elizabeth contemplated his words, but made no comment. Gloucester was young, but not too young to have a mistress, and here at court such things were arranged when they did not occur naturally. Hastings provided women for the King's bed as readily as the court purveyors secured meat, and no doubt he would be equally happy to serve the King's brother. It would be interesting to know whether Gloucester was ploughing his own furrow or simply being accommodated; but it was unlikely that her curiosity on the subject would be rewarded.

Margaret Beaufort had produced a piece of needlework from some crevice. Bending over it, her eyes obviously struggling in the uncertain light, she carefully inserted a couple of stitches before speaking again. 'I've heard that the King intends that Gloucester shall marry a daughter of the French King.' she said to Elizabeth. 'It seems the alliance with Burgundy is not quite what Edward's advisers hoped it would be.' There was a further long pause, while more stitches went in and sufficient time passed to make it clear that Elizabeth did not intend to answer. 'So, it seems we shall have peace after all, instead of war. One can only pray that it will be so, for the safety of our husbands and of other good Englishmen; although such a peace will scarcely aid the cause of our exiled Beaufort kinsmen.'

'They have no cause, as far as I know,' Elizabeth said. She was already growing impatient with the conversation.

'Our family has scarcely been advanced by the rule of York,' Margaret answered, her voice casual as she made another stitch. Her eyes flicked to Elizabeth and Buckingham successively, as if she wished to remind them of the share of Beaufort blood in their veins.

Buckingham grinned. 'Well, dear Aunt, at least I have gained my most noble wife.' He paused, a mischievous light in his eyes. 'I wonder if Dickon knows what his brother has planned for him. I must ask him in the morning – we've promised each other an hour of tennis. The news might put him off his game.'

Elizabeth was surprised by the underlying note of malice in the boy's voice. She suspected Harry Buckingham was one who enjoyed stirring trouble for others and taking advantage for himself. Perhaps, she thought, he will grow out of it once he takes a man's responsibilities on his shoulders.

She longed to be away from this place with its gossip and vile intrigues; longed to be home at Framlingham, free to ride out in fresh air. Free to mourn her sister.

Eleanor had been tricked, betrayed, dishonoured. The King was to blame, with Hastings his willing accomplice. She burned for vengeance, but there was nothing she could do about it. Even to speak of the matter, to hint, was dangerous. Hastings' tone, as much as his words, had reminded her of that.

The music drew to its straggling conclusion, and the dancers reverenced one another and either turned to conversation or went their separate ways. Most of them were red-flushed from the vigour of their exercise, but the musicians were already tempting them to begin anew. This time the tune was slow and stately, befitting the gentler, more formal steps of the basse dance.

About the author

Brian Wainwright developed, in his teens, a particular fascination with the era of Richard II, another king he believes history has sadly misjudged. There were few novels about that period and Brian eventually came across *White Boar* by Marian Palmer, which started him off on his fascination with the Third Richard. His main focus remains with the House of York throughout its existence.

Brian's first published novel, *The Adventures of Alianore Audley*, set in the Yorkist era, was produced by way of light relief during a lull in the long task of researching and writing *Within the Fetterlock*. Brian was surprised by the number of people who appear to enjoy what he admits is his fairly eccentric sense of humour.

Within the Fetterlock was an entirely different sort of project, one that has verged on an obsession. Brian was fascinated by Constance of York almost from the first time he found a reference to her existence, and the novel was whittled down from many previous attempts.

After a long break from writing, Brian is currently working on a prequel to *Within the Fetterlock*, entitled *This New Spring of Time*, and he has longer-term plans for a serious Ricardian novel.

Website:	https://brianwainwright.blogspot.com/
Amazon:	https://www.amazon.co.uk/Brian-Wainwright/e/B001K8RUQS/
Facebook:	https://www.facebook.com/Alianore-Audley-287530691257592/
	https://www.facebook.com/ThisNewSpringofTime/

If Only...

Alex Marchant

'Lady Eleanor Butler?'

I search my memory, trying to recall the lady of whom he speaks. But, though the name tugs at the edges of my mind, I have to admit defeat.

'Who is – was she, brother?'

His face bears a look I rarely see upon it – discomfort, embarrassment even. But at what?

'She was a lady I – I met. Once or twice.'

'Once or twice? Why then is her death so important?'

'Important?' His laugh is strained, an attempt at light-heartedness. 'Maybe it is not – not really. And it was so long ago.'

'Long ago?' Now my perplexity is heightened. 'Hers is not a recent death? There are no legal matters that require urgent attention?'

'No, indeed – it is some years ago now – I do not quite recall how many. No, perhaps – perhaps it is no matter at all.'

'No matter? It is surely a great matter if you should summon me the length of England to attend you at such short notice.'

Has impatience crept into my voice? I abandoned important work at home in the north to respond to his summons. Yet though he is my brother, he is also King of England. I must be careful in my words, my tone. I must not offend. I must not try his patience – like George.

But, if he hears aught in my speech, he does not heed it. He throws his arm about my shoulders. His great bear-like arm. It is all I can do to stop myself recoiling from the stab of pain it causes. I must not remind him of it, the curve in my back that continues to grow, lest he fears I can no longer serve him so well. But he does not notice, as he draws me to the deep-recessed window. He stands silent for a time, staring out at the teeming traffic on the Thames, while I steal a glance askance at him. His eyes, usually so clear, so merry, are brooding, cloudy like the sky reflected in the busy waterway.

He speaks again, gazing still, but perhaps not seeing.

'There is none I trust so well as you, little brother.'

I smile at his words. That he should still call me that, even now I am no longer a boy, but a full-grown man. Though, to be sure, I will never now reach his stature. He stands a full head and more above me, as he clasps me so close to him I almost feel, rather than hear, his next words

'You have ever proved true, Richard – throughout all my many trials. And now, now I must have a witness – witnesses – whom I trust completely. No one else must ever know.'

'Witnesses? To what?'

Silence. For a second. As his grip tightens, as his lips tighten. Then...

'Elizabeth is not happy. She says there is no need. That we should continue as before. That nothing need change. That no one need know. But I ...'

This sudden mention of his wife. The queen. Why...?

'But I – I fear for my son. What may happen if ... His right to the throne must be secure if I should die while he is yet young.'

First, talk of his wife. Now of his son. Young Edward. My bafflement is no less. Why does he speak like this? Of such a thing as his death? He is young still himself – in his prime, at least. And why such worry about the succession?

I do not speak, but he blunders on, his eyes fixed still on the distant river. A feverishness tinges their depths.

'How could I ride to battle again in the knowledge that ... Before now – at Barnet, Tewkesbury – I knew you or George could – would succeed me should I fall on the battlefield. That a Plantagenet king would continue to rule in my stead, though he were my brother, not my son. But now ... now my son is born, is my heir – now it would be his right to rule. But – but he must be legitimate...'

Understanding strikes me like a blow from a halberd. This puzzle he has skirted round. The lady he spoke of, this Eleanor Butler...

She – she he had wed before ... before he wed Elizabeth...

Elizabeth. The queen. Yet ... not ... not his queen. For the Lady Eleanor still lived until – when? Some years at least after my brother's marriage to the mother of his children. That marriage that had itself been secret – and against the wishes of Parliament, of our cousin Warwick. When a foreign alliance had been needed, a foreign princess prepared – a princess then spurned when news of this marriage to Elizabeth emerged.

And now? Now he seeks a second marriage ceremony – as secret as that first – with witnesses he can trust not to tell...

Or rather – a third ceremony as secret as both those 'marriages'... secret in the world, but known before God...

My mind whirls, my world in turmoil. All the certainties of my life dropping away one by one. Darkness spins my thoughts around, clouds befog my sight. I close my eyelids, a defence against the hammering reality.

*

'Your Grace? King Richard? It's time to wake.'

The words, the voice, though quiet, slice through my reverie. But they do not wake me into the grey glimmer of the dawn.

For I was not asleep.

But I raise my head from the silk pillow as though it were heavy with slumber, as though brushing away the gentle touch of dreams.

My attendants and gentlemen must not know I had been awake. They must not think I have slept ill. In truth, indeed, my sleep was like a babe's this night – till I was stirred by the first cock crow in the village nearest to the royal camp. And then I lay a while, raking across the events of my life so far. Events that brought me to this dawn, this day of reckoning. When I must face he who would take my crown – once my brother's crown – that should have been our father's – and perhaps ... perhaps also my brother's son's.

And I thought of how that life might have been so different if – if only...

If only my brother had summoned me the length of England one day, some years ago...

About the author

Alex Marchant was born and raised in the rolling Surrey downs, but, following stints as an archaeologist and in publishing in London and Gloucester, now lives surrounded by moors in King Richard III's northern heartland, not far from his beloved York and Middleham.

A Ricardian and writer since a teenager, Alex's first novel, *Time out of Time*, won the 2012 Chapter One Children's Book Award, but was then put on the backburner in 2013 at the announcement of the rediscovery of King Richard's grave in a car park in Leicester. Discovering that there were no books for children telling the story of the real Richard III, Alex was inspired to write them, and so *The Order of the White Boar* and its sequel, *The King's Man*, were born. Together they tell King Richard's story through the eyes of a young page who enters his service in the summer of 1482, and have been called 'a wonderful work of historical fiction for both children and adults' by the *Bulletin* of the Richard III Society and 'exciting, appealing and refreshing' by the publication of Richard III's Loyal Supporters (www.r3loyalsupporters.com).

Alex's third book in the *White Boar* sequence, *King in Waiting*, will be published in 2021 and *Time out of Time* is being reworked for publication.

Website:	https://alexmarchantblog.wordpress.com
Amazon:	https://www.amazon.co.uk/Alex-Marchant/e/B075JJKX8W/
Facebook:	https://www.facebook.com/AlexMarchantAuthor/
Twitter:	https://twitter.com/AlexMarchant84
GoodReads:	https://www.goodreads.com/author/show/17175168.Alex_Marchant

The Play's the Thing

Kit Mareska

Westminster Abbey, 1845

There is an art to sitting convincingly when one is between lives. Of course, Richard III isn't truly *sitting* in the Coronation Chair – we ghosts have no need. Yet he hovers close enough that I see no space between the oak's chipped paint and schoolboy graffiti and his ermine-lined robe, its purple deepened by his faint blue glow. I cannot help but admire his mastery of illusion. But then, my villain has been dead even longer than I.

As if his choice of seat weren't enough to remind me that he was king three hundred and sixty years ago, he is also wearing a gem-encrusted crown. His brown hair holds none of the grey that mine does.

I bow low, noting the cast of my pink-hazed feet against the black and white marble tiles.

'You may rise, Master Shakespeare.'

Not a northern accent. Richard's speech was well set before he went to live in Yorkshire. But there is still a hint of old pronunciation, the way his tongue wants to lend a third syllable to my name.

I straighten, glad that I chose a stiff ruff in which to meet him, and richer fabrics than those I wore when bent over my table, my pen struggling to keep pace with my thoughts.

'I am honoured by your summons, Your Grace. I thought you had adopted a policy of ignoring my presence.'

'I was not ignoring you, sir. I was waiting to ensure that my reaction was not over-hasty. I have condemned certain men too quickly in the past.'

'Talk you of . . .' *killing* leaps to my lips; I swallow it: '. . . condemnation?'

He abruptly stands, his form shifting. The slight hill of his right shoulder becomes a mountain that nearly bends him double. While his face does not *age,* it sharpens, its grooves growing more pronounced, its teeth more like fangs.

'You distorted the events of my life,' he rasps. 'Laid all manner of crimes at my feet, then called it history. *This* is how you portrayed me. No matter that, were this so, I could never have hefted a weapon, much less wielded one through three battles!'

He resumes his former shape, but leaves the robe and crown behind. He now wears only a blue velvet doublet which allows me to see that, even though he *could* align his shoulders perfectly, he does not.

The space that once held my belly feels oddly alight, considering that I can vanish into thin air at any time. Nothing holds me here except curiosity. Richard is the only one of my characters ever to confront me.

'Your Highness, those were merely stories! They do not matter, do not alter the truth. *There is nothing good or bad but thinking makes it so.*'

'You relish the sound of your own words, Master Shakespeare.'

I assume my most Puckish smile. 'I cannot help myself. They are good words.'

'Here are some more for you, then: *Life holds every man dear, but the dear man holds honour far more precious than life.*'

Hectored with my own Hector. Whatever I might say about Richard's family, there was not a dullard among them.

He says, 'Another on which I have spent much thought over the centuries: *No legacy is so rich as honesty.*'

Will this end well? I kick my doubts away. There is no violence here. We are little more than light.

'I am flattered by your attention to my scribblings, Your Grace.'

'I have leisure for such things now.'

'It *is* pleasant, such a slow pace, is it not?'

'I hate it.'

The bald humanity of his confession would steal my breath, had I any.

He floats forward from the Coronation Chair.

'Let us walk.'

That verb, too, is a misnomer. There are no footfalls from his boots. I, however, take delight in moving my legs, following a pace behind as he drifts up the nave's south aisle, then passes through the quire and turns right at the transept, into a crowd of tourists.

I welcome contact with the living who, for all their blindness, can sometimes feel me. Richard, on the other hand, dodges them, even leaping aside when a child stops short.

To go to such lengths . . . *'tis passing strange.*

'Why do you linger between lives, Master Shakespeare?' he asks, recovering from his leap.

The decision to move into one's next life is the most private and personal one we have. Perhaps he has not *been* a person in so long, he forgets this.

I parry his intrusion lightly.

'For the eavesdropping, Your Grace. The language that exists now – some of my own words and phrases have entered into everyday use. I never knew it so pleasing to be common.'

As we enter Poet's Corner, he says, 'This is not the monument of a common man.'

Indeed. My monument is the most prominent one. In marble the colour of buttermilk, the life-sized me leans on a podium, one leg casually crossed over the other, looking entirely satisfied.

I turn away from it, venting a small nasal huff.

'What is wrong, Master Shakespeare? Do you not find the statue flattering?'

Is he goading? No. His brow is drawn, his confusion sincere.

Reluctantly, I spin back towards myself.

'The portrait is . . . fine. The sculptor shaved a few pounds off my frame, even if he bestowed no more hair on my dome. But there is a *misprint*' – I wave an accusatory arm at the scroll that hangs off the podium – 'so grievous that I can hardly bear to look – *haven't* looked, since I made the hideous discovery at its unveiling a hundred years ago.'

Richard reads but betrays no enlightenment.

'The sculptor got the word wrong,' I snap. 'It should be "the fabric of *this* vision", not "*a* vision". *A* vision has no music!' I clench my hands, wishing I had a script to throw at the sculptor. Just as well that my actual body lies at Stratford.

The king clearly does not grasp the magnitude of this catastrophe. His gaze veers from the scroll down the podium itself.

Of course. *This* is the reason he led me here. Not to commiserate over my tragedy.

The base of the podium has three faces carved into it: Queen Elizabeth's, King Henry V's, and Richard's own.

'Well . . . this is awkward,' I manage.

Language, thou fickle bitch – deserting me when I need you so.

'Quite,' the king agrees drily. 'I can't decide which vexes me more: that your knee presses into my brow or that I look more like Henry Tudor than myself.'

The glowing blue form by my side has a less oppressed nose, an outraged chin and flashing eyes.

'This wasn't even crafted until more than a hundred years after my passing. I had nothing to do with its design, Your Grace!'

'Did you not? You are supported by your greatest patron, your greatest hero . . . and your greatest villain. Do you think I would have been cast thusly if not for you?'

Actually, I consider Iago my greatest villain. But the sculptor chose to feature real people, two of whom are entombed in this very abbey.

'*Reputation is an idle and most false imposition, oft got without merit and lost without deserving.* I offer my apology, King Richard, if my words have done you injustice.'

'*If* they have done me injustice? I was not responsible for my brother Clarence's death. Neither did I bring about the end of Henry VI. Ask him yourself. He drifts around still. Canterbury, if not Windsor.'

'Unnecessary, Your Grace. The souls of men are church windows. When they lie, their colour grows clouded. Your blue is clear.'

He jerks, his jaw falling. 'So simple a test?'

'I've always found it so. Though, why *do* you choose such a deep cast? Surely you remember that it represented mourning in your time.' My pink is far more cheerful.

'I . . . chose the colour of my son's eyes. He and his mother left me only recently.'

'They stayed with you a good long time, then. My son proceeded to his next life before I ever arrived here, and my wife did not tarry long.'

With a last bitter glance at my monument, the king drifts backward, beyond Henry V's effigy and Edward the Confessor's chapel to that of his own destroyer.

Frugal though he'd been, Henry Tudor spared no expense on the place of his burial. It is like standing beneath an elaborate wedding cake that has been tipped upside-down, its lacy sugar about to melt on to my head.

But its drips are trapped in gold. A spectacular work. Makes me long for sweets every time.

Richard floats toward the effigy of his niece, Tudor's queen. The one he is said to have murdered his wife to marry.

'Is she as you remember?' I ask.

He has lost such tells as blushing or quickening of breath, having been *between* so long. Instead, his velvet doublet fades away, leaving the same shirt in which he might sleep. Yet his eyes are a calm sea as he says, 'It isn't possible to capture her love of family in bronze. But her kindness . . . of that, there is a hint.'

His eyes stray to her husband beside her, and his upper lip flutters in a sneer. Then his shoulders square beneath their linen and he passes through a wall to the right.

I follow, into a chamber that is narrower but no less fine. And holds the tomb of Tudor's granddaughter.

Elizabeth.

Titania.

Perfectly curled wig, impossibly crisp ruff, jewels that do nothing to soften the sharp nose. Sceptre in her long right fingers, orb in her left. Her Majesty's hands were the loveliest that ever applauded me.

The king allows me a moment, then he rolls like a storm cloud over to a stout marble urn whose sharp-cornered design holds nothing of humanity. Certainly nothing of boyhood. He translates the urn's Latin aloud.

'Here lie the relics of Edward V, King of England, and Richard, Duke of York. These brothers being confined in the Tower of London, and there stifled with pillows, were privately and meanly buried, by the order of their perfidious uncle, *Richard the Usurper* . . .'

He whirls on me, larger than before.

'Do you still mean to tell me that your words have no lasting effect? I was crowned under this roof with God's blessing – and *this* is how I'm described, as a usurper and a murderer of children! I had hoped that your false charges would fade with the years. That the good I tried to do would be all that remained. A vain hope, perhaps, but vanity is the least of what we carry with us. I underestimated, though, the way that your Hamlet, your Lear, your Falstaff have become characters that the world is unwilling to forget. All those who knew me have passed. When today's people imagine me, it is as a hunchbacked monster, crazed with greed and schemes.'

'*The evil that men do lives after them, the good is oft interred with their bones.* I was not the one who induced your unfortunate transformation, however. That began soon after Henry Tudor took your throne.'

'You may not have been the first, but you were the worst. No one has done my reputation more damage. *You* made poetry of infamy. *You* had me lurching about on stage for people to see with their own eyes and mock with their own tongues. You did it for fame. And money.'

My villain sees me as *his* villain.

Were I in the midst of writing, I would lean back in my chair, lost in revelation until my dripping pen besmirched my paper. But he is waiting. Glaring.

'Money *is* a matter of survival, Your Grace. I had a family to feed. Barely scraping by with one child, then God bestowed *twins* upon us.'

'I have tried to recall such concerns these long years. Tried to forgive you and not let your portrait bother me. But you have, indeed, turned this time of rest and retrospection into the winter of my discontent. I cannot move on while the injury goes unaddressed.'

'*Hell is empty and all the devils are here.* Are we not addressing your injury now?'

'In order for there to be justice, there must also be a *re*-dressing. I am going to punish you, Master Shakespeare.'

I have no pulse to quicken, no saliva to dry. Only endless time to stare at a poised axe.

Yet, what can he do – decry one of my sonnets? I've never died of a critic's wounds, can hardly start now.

'Before I pronounce sentence, however . . . I have been thinking on what you said of clarity. And your pink was somewhat clouded earlier. I should like to know the real reason you linger between lives.'

The request is politely phrased, for all his fury and resentment. But what he asks . . . I shy away as though it were Hell's mouth. I do not wish to shine a torch there, nor drop a stone to gauge its depth. I want no part of it.

Yet, I have wronged him. Treated his niece and nephews, his honour and dignity as prey. I owe him, more dearly than ever I owed the grocer.

My gaze seeks the soaring stained-glass window above us.

'What if . . . what if I cannot write in the next life? You'll know the rumours: that we leave all memory of our former selves behind, become blank canvases awaiting new splashes of colour.'

'What colour of your soul is art, poet? Red? Yellow?'

'Writing is the leaden grey frame that holds all my colours together. Which is why I cannot risk its loss.'

He smiles slightly, waiting for . . .

The joyous lightning that slams into my brain.

'Oh, Your Grace – how right you are! The frame we carry through! I can move on. I shall *always* write. How can I not have seen it before?'

'Fear is the heaviest of curtains. When it drops on you, you cannot help but stumble blindly.'

Without meaning to, I have floated upward, my pink blazing so that it purples the edge of his blue glow.

I settle back to the floor.

'Whose words are those? Not mine. Yours?'

He smiles sadly, briefly, in acknowledgement.

'There remains the matter of punishment.'

'Of course, Your Grace. Although now it will land no harder than a mother's kiss.'

I shall write forever and ever, six lives or sixty, however long it takes to polish this flawed soul of mine into a perfect –

'Do not be so sure. For I mean to plant the notion that your plays, Master Shakespeare . . . were written by someone else.'

'Who?' I quip through the peculiar heat that is sweeping upward from my belly. 'George Peele? Thomas Middleton? Ben Jonson if you must. Just do not make it Kit Marlowe. I owe him from a game of cards, but not so much as that.'

'I am serious, sir.'

He is. He –

Oh, God!

He is.

The spreading heat explodes like a star, leaving me encased in ice.

In blackness.

My shape is gone, my light. My words . . .

I have no words. Only keening. And gasps. And dry wild sobs.

A woman walks into the chapel, the swishing of her skirts and the untinged paleness of her skin proclaiming her living status. Her eyes go to the ceiling and widen. She takes two open-mouthed steps further, then stops.

I am too shattered to tolerate her gentle wonder.

Get out.

Her head turns, searching. Her gloved hands rub her upper arms. For all her clothing and all her distraction, she heard me.

GET OUT!!!

With a swirling of silk, she flees, leaving me a husk.

I gradually resume form, and even then lack all hue and such details as the ruff. Or feet.

'Please, Your Grace. Choose anything else – *anything!*'

'*The miserable have no other medicine.*'

'Measure for Measure'. Seems no comedy now.

'Besides,' he drawls, 'as you so consoled me earlier, it will merely be a story. Will not matter, will not alter the truth . . .'

Oh, wicked villainy!

My hands flap like headed chickens, then clutch each other in hope.

'You said you *mean* to plant this rumour . . . Then it is not done yet?'

'It is delicate, draining work to commune with the living. I have made the beginnings of a connection, but have not yet been able to send the full suspicion. I should be able to, given time. I do not expect many to believe, but even a few –'

'*One* person's belief would be too many. Please! *I'll kneel down, and ask forgiveness: so we'll live, and pray, and sing, and tell old tales.*' I throw myself down, pressing my brow into his knee, blathering like Polonius.

'No.'

'But *why*? Why this? You have made me heartily sorry. It still does not change the past, nor will this plan.'

'Did you not write that *What is past is prologue*? If I can shake men's faith in your genius, perhaps I can shake their faith in my evil. Until I try, I am not free to move on. Loyalty is the frame that holds *me* together. Those were never mere words.'

'There are no such things as "mere words" to a writer.' I shake my head, a gesture I had thought lost, but now that I feel so humanly powerless it comes racing back. 'I still don't understand.'

His voice sinks and his shoulders sag.

'Then I will show you one more place.'

Working my legs is beyond me now. I ooze like blood. Back toward the ornate tomb of Edward the Confessor.

Richard aims not for the saint's tomb, however, but a much smaller one, black-lidded and tucked into a low niche.

His hands tremble against it.

'I was far beyond making decisions about a casket when she died. Was barely able to get out of bed, even though there was no more solace for me in that soft place. I couldn't read through the seeping tears, had no idea what I signed, only wanted to satisfy my council so that they would let me return to bed and draw its curtains closed. So Anne Neville, the lively, laughing woman who was my wife and my queen – and my friend – was laid to rest in this plain, unmarked tomb. Less than a year after we laid our son Ned in his.'

He is more than touching the stone now. His hands have sunk in, as have his brow and part of his left shoulder, so desperate is he to connect to what remains of the woman inside. And . . . his clothes are gone.

He died at thirty-two. He is lean and, turned as he is, I see not only the height difference between his shoulders but that his spine has a drastic C-shaped curve in its midst. So much pain in a single letter.

I would cry foul – too obvious, too over-reaching a ploy – but for one thing: his right arm, his sword arm. It is well muscled. Not the withered thing that some witnesses claimed he brandished at that fateful council meeting. If he were playing for my sympathy, why not include that second deformity?

Unless . . . unless he is being . . .

Real.

Is it possible?

The crown. The robe. Not to strike awe, just so that I would recognize him, since he is so far from who I portrayed? He shed them nearly at once.

The Coronation Chair: where no one else would sit. Where he'd be out of the way of the contact he takes care to avoid – because it disturbs the living, not because it disturbs him.

The clarity of his colour all along.

The way he did not want to bring me to his wife, only doing so when I left him no choice. He sought – fought for – my understanding, knowing I shall write again.

He means to do this horrible thing, yes. But first he gave me the key to a new life where his punishment may not even matter.

No. It shall *always* matter. Those works are my soul.

Yet, can I call his wrath unjustified? If he did *none* of it?

An honest man. Who died because he was thrust into a court of veteran game players, when he himself played none.

Real.

God help me.

God help us both.

' . . . planned to choose something more fitting for her, something splendid and surprising that conjured life rather than death, once I was able to say her name without it buckling me. Henry Tudor invaded before that day came. So here she is, forever. An anonymous afterthought. But at least she's *here.* Our son – our son's body is as misplaced as my own.'

He pulls himself loose, turning to me. A smattering of hairs graces his breast, as well as a couplet of faded scars.

'Ned died at Middleham while Anne and I were away at court. He'd never been hale, but we hadn't suspected just how . . . The guilt crushed her. I suspect she welcomed the consumption that rushed her to his side – and it *was* disease, poet. *Not* poison. Years after I joined them, Ned asked to visit his body. Anne and I conducted him. Except . . . he was not where we had buried him. Wasn't *anywhere*.'

He wipes at an eye. But tears do not rise in us, much less fall.

'Ned was not especially disturbed; he was a joyful spirit, eager to move on, having been cheated of a full previous life. But Anne . . . like the consumption all over again . . . I didn't even know to fear that here . . . and I knew that the disregard shown to Ned's body was because of me. And men like you. He was a king's son! Would himself have been king!

'My bold girl . . . I could not watch her waste away a second time, and even though we longed to stay together, there was no question of letting Ned transition alone again. I sent them forward, promising to follow soon. I've combed every inch of Middleham Castle, every church. I cannot find him. Cannot feel him. Our poor boy . . .'

I could have written something more quotable. Not more heartfelt.

He that dies pays all debts.

I've apologized to Richard already. I owe him . . . a confession.

A baring.

Once more unto the breach, dear friends.

'I am a writer, my lord. I am a writer before I am anything else: Englishman, husband . . . even father. I loved my son – of course! – but Hamnet's death did not destroy me. Did not even put me off my comedies more than a few days. If anyone could share claim to such an all-encompassing occupation, it would be a king. Yet here you are, postponing a new start for the sake of two people who may no longer even know you. I am selfish. I would not surrender a single sonnet for anyone. Yet, for all my words, I cannot talk you out of this, can I? Against hatred I might stand a chance. Against such love . . .' My second head shake in a century. 'Nor do I deserve to.'

He answers one lifelike gesture with another: a shrug.

'I only know that I cannot move on without doing *something* for them. This plan is the first glimmer of hope I've had since they left, and I shall see it through.'

I was an actor as well as a writer. And an actor knows when to exit.

I bow once more.

'I wish you good fortune, then, Your Grace, in one quest if not the other. If you will forgive my mixing plays . . . *Farewell, fair cruelty*. May thy crown be called content.'

Richard III inclines his head, regal even in nudity.

'Farewell, Master Bard.'

Grief

Joanne R. Larner

Your laughter stalks the secret recesses of my mind,
Echoing around the hollow void.
I grasp desperately at a glimpse of your hair,
Fair like the sun on wheat,
Your eyes the blue of speedwell...

Speed well, my son ... every thought reminds me,
Brings me back to the cold, terrifying truth: You are gone.
Your mirth a memory, fading, to my dread,
Despite my mind's attempts to clutch it back.

I am a mighty king, yet powerless to reverse the loss of your
    loving gaze
That used to warm me in the icy depths of a frigid Yorkshire
    winter.
All is frozen in an eternal winter now.

I panic at the vanishing essence of you, intangible, elusive.
Unbearable, the thought of never more hearing your
    mischievous giggle.

You knew my stern reprimands were half-hearted,
Saw the loving twinkle in my regal eye.
I, ever your passive accomplice in defiance of your mother.

Your mother, who grieves so deeply I despair of ever
    rescuing her
From the bottomless well of desolation she has entered.
I know not how to salvage the tattered remnants of her mind,
Just as I was helpless to save the life of my child, my hopes.

I would surrender all the rich, empty trappings of kingship
To once more cradle you in my arms.

I have the crazed wish to turn back the clock;
The insane thought that had I been there,
A father instead of a king, you would live still.

I must go on, I know it – for the realm.
I must entertain, wear a mask of jollity,
Attend to the running of the state.
Yet now, what was once a joy to me is reduced to this:

The arduous, empty burden of a king.

About the author

Joanne R. Larner lives in Rayleigh, Essex, with her husband, John, and two dogs, Jonah, the black lab cross and Hunter, the miniature dachshund. She has worked as an osteopath for more than twenty years, but always wanted to write and was inspired to achieve her ambition by Richard III.

Joanne read every book she could find on the subject of the last Plantagenet king, but became tired of knowing how they would end, so she finally decided to write her own – a time-travel alternative history called *Richard Liveth Yet*, the 'book she wanted to read'. This has since become a trilogy with the addition of *Richard Liveth Yet: A Foreign Country* and *Richard Liveth Yet: Hearts Never Change*. She has also collaborated with Susan Lamb on two humorous books about Richard: *Dickon's Diaries* and *Dickon's Diaries 2* – a madcap mixture of medieval and modern, a cross between the humour of the *Carry On* films and *The Two Ronnies*. Larner and Lamb recently published a magazine-style edition in the same vein: *Ye Muddleham Sunne*. Joanne has also completed a new novel about Richard III: *Distant Echoes: Richard III Speaks!*

Her next venture will be a factual account of her own psychic and spiritual journey, incorporating hints and tips for developing your own psychic potential and a few spiritual experiences concerning Richard III himself. It will be called *The Fox and the Lion*.

Website:	https://www.joannelarner.wordpress.com
Amazon:	https://www.amazon.co.uk/Joanne-R-Larner/e/B00XO1IC4S
Facebook:	https://www.facebook.com/JoanneRLarner
	https://www.facebook.com/RichardLivethYet
Twitter:	https://www.twitter.com/JetBlackJo

The Silent Boy

Nicola Slade

An adapted excerpt from *The House at Ladywell*

'You're home, then, Kat?' The farmer raised his head from his tankard and gave the newcomer a jaundiced look. 'Not caught a husband yet?'

'Is that what you hoped, Pa?' She looked down her long nose, so like his own, her light-brown eyes flashing. 'You should have thought of that before you sent me away. There was a sad lack of husbands on offer at that damned convent.'

As her father drained the last drop of ale, Katherine's eyes softened and she clapped him on the shoulder.

'I was sorry to hear about Joan and the bull, Pa. You'd have thought she'd have more sense than to walk across the field when he was in a fine old temper and she in the family way.'

'Ah, well.' He reached up to squeeze her hand. 'The truth is, Kat, I can't be doing with yet another new wife in the house. I thought 'twould be easy to get a son, but first your mother, God rest her sainted soul . . .' He crossed himself, looking sentimental. 'She did her best, but all she rose to was a clutch of sickly girls and you, m'dear, the only one to survive.'

'Poor old Pa. You had bad luck, didn't you? Who expected Bess to die in childbirth and the baby with her? And Joan was another buxom wench. So I'm to stay at home now, am I? No more attempts to get me off your hands?'

'Ah now, 'twas never for that reason, Kat, as you well know.' He cracked a faint smile. 'It was more than my life was worth to have you and Bess together in the house that you'd managed while your Ma ailed. The convent was a good enough plan then. We'd heard rumours about His Grace the King and his quarrels with the clergy, but who'd have guessed it would go the way it has.' He pushed himself up from the table to reveal broad thighs and a large belly. 'A clever girl like you might have risen to Mother Superior, not be thrown out with all the rest when some jumped-up clerk bought the place.'

'So I might have done,' she nodded. 'The convent was a shambles. I'd have had the accounts straight in no time, but Mother Superior said if I was keen on bookwork, I could help with the missal they planned for the bishop. Tcha!' she snorted indignantly. 'With rats running free in the granary, prodigious waste in the kitchens, and four legs in some of the beds at night . . . I've missed it here so much. Nigh on five years wasted.' She heaved a sigh, skewering him with a frown. 'What's happened here, Pa? The thatch is rotten, there's a tree growing out of the chimney and windows boarded up. 'Tis hardly fit for the pigs. What's to become of us here at the farm – and the holy well and the chapel too?'

'Ah, that.' He looked sheepish. 'The fellow acting for the king's commissioner rode by a couple of months past. He said he'd come to take a look over here.' He shrugged. 'Seems nobody gave a thought to the chapel in the priory sale, so I offered to buy it all – the chapel, the well, the land and this house too – so we shook on it.'

'But that's good news, Pa, great news.' She hugged him. 'What are your plans? What about the monks at the chapel here?'

'Ah . . .' He looked at his feet. 'I can't turn out those old fellows, can I? Brother Dominic sits by the fire all a-tremble, Brother Anselm's near-blind and Brother Rohan don't know Michaelmas from Monday, 'tis all one to him.'

*

Next morning Katherine dragged her father out to survey the farm.

'To think we have His Grace's lusty antics to thank for my release from bondage,' she sighed, as she steered him towards the river. 'Mother always said no good would come of his goings-on with that Bullen whore, and look what became of the wench these three years gone.'

'Hold hard, girl.' Dickon Wellman wheezed along in his daughter's train, but when he reached a gnarled rowan tree he put out a hand to support himself. 'Funny thing,' he said, staring up at the greening boughs and picturing the froth of snowy blossom to come in May, 'my old grandfather told me there's always been a rowan tree here. This one stands strong yet, and when it's old, another must be planted. Dire bad luck, he said, were the tree not renewed. You remember that, Kat.'

'You know I will, Pa.'

She followed him as he made his way to a fallen tree trunk and they sat in companionable silence, enjoying the unexpected March sunshine.

'What do you mean to do with the chapel, Pa?'

'I'll pull it down,' he said. 'The well-house too. I've a mind to build a fine new house with the stones, right here. What do you reckon?'

'A house?' She stood up to examine the ground. Her eyes shone. 'I like that idea. But can we afford it, Pa?'

'Never you mind, Kat.' He looked smug and tapped the side of his nose. 'The king's man was no farmer. He had no more idea of the value of this land than one of our sheep, so when I put in a paltry offer he didn't have the wits to ask for more. I couldn't believe it when he said the place was mine. Nobody wanted it, he said. The townsfolk only wanted the priory church, so the smallholdings and granges were being sold off piecemeal.'

The complacent smile faded from his large ruddy face.

'The farm is in good shape, but I'm sorry about the house. I've had this idea in mind since we first heard that Master Cromwell and His Grace had their sights on the monks' wealth, so I set my mind to it that I'd buy the land and the chapel and build if I got the chance. And hark, Kat,' he rumbled, 'you're past nineteen, and a woman with a tidy bit of land will need a man's protection when I'm gone.'

*

The next day Katherine went to the chapel to greet the old men she had loved since childhood.

'Well, Brother Anselm,' she said, sitting between him and Brother Dominic, whose shoulders trembled under her gentle embrace. Brother Rohan, in his corner, paid no heed, singing tunelessly to the fat tabby on his knee. 'What think you of Pa's notion to build a new house?'

'A fine idea,' two of the old men chorused, the one head nodding more than ever, while the other's sightless eyes closed in contemplation of glories he would never see.

'Your father is a hardworking man and a kind one,' quavered Brother Dominic, adding hopefully, 'Master Dickon did promise he would never put us out of house and home, and glad we were to hear that, for what would become of the three of us else? There's precious little we can do but pray.'

'Prayers are always welcome, brother,' she assured him. 'Pa and I will be glad of your company wherever we live. I do wish, though, that I had someone to help design this house.'

'You need Brother Ambrosius,' Brother Anselm said. 'He's away to Winchester hoping to wheedle some money out of the bishop for our needs. He used to oversee our little infirmary once a week till we had word to disband. But there, Master Dickon will see all's right.'

'Aye,' the blind monk chuckled. 'Ambrosius hared off to give the bishop a piece of his mind.'

'Ambrosius should get married,' Brother Rohan cackled. 'A fine young fellow needs a rich wife, better for him than a priory any day.'

*

Katherine's hands were full, leaving her no time to fume about her father's hints.

'You do as you please,' he told her. 'I'm no hand at fripperies.' He blew his nose loudly. 'I lost heart for building a house anew with no son to follow, but Old Harry goes a-wenching and here you are, home again. As for this fine new house,' he patted her on the back and laughed as she buckled slightly at the knees, 'all I ask for are high ceilings for I'm a large fellow, and a fine big room with a handsome fireplace to sit beside on a winter's night. Aye, with a fine bedchamber above it, so I can die in grand comfort when the time comes!'

As she approached the chapel, Katherine was surprised to hear the sound of an axe, accompanied by a cheerful baritone.

A half-naked young giant swung the axe in time to his song as he split a tree trunk into logs. At Katherine's involuntary gasp, he looked up and lost his rhythm.

'For the love of God, woman,' he shouted, as he flung down his axe. 'I nearly chopped my own bloody leg off. Have you no more sense than to distract a man when he's at work?'

'Don't you dare speak to me like that,' she snapped, trying to steady her breathing. The axe had landed perilously close to his leg. 'You should take more care. There's no infirmarian to see to you now.'

'Not true.' His mouth twisted in a smile. She blinked as the black eyes narrowed into amused slits and his face creased, revealing through the dark stubble a pair of dimples any maiden would covet. 'I'd just have to issue instructions about cauterizing the stump and keeping it clean.' He hitched his habit back up over his shoulders. 'Brother Ambrosius,' he said. 'Lately infirmarian of this place. Do I address our landlord's daughter?'

'I thought you'd gone to Winchester,' Katherine stammered.

He glowered. 'My trip achieved precious little, nor did I expect it to.'

'What will you do?'

'I can build your father's grand house,' he said cheerfully. 'I hear you need a man of vision to tell the masons what needs to be done. I have a turn for such work, and here I am without a job and at your service, Mistress Katherine.'

'I'd be grateful indeed, Brother Ambrosius,' she replied. 'Pa wants his two grand rooms, one above the other, and he cares naught for the rest of the house, leaving it all in my hands.'

'Call me Hugh,' he said. 'With no tonsure and a beard,' he rubbed his chin and grinned ruefully as it rasped, 'Brother Ambrosius may safely be left behind. Hugh Beauchamp must take his place, though I may have to work on that too, for Beauchamps hold no high place in King Henry's heart.'

*

Within a week Hugh and Katherine had hammered out a plan, with Dickon's approval, and Hugh spent much of one whole day pacing the proposed site.

'Stand here with me at the front door.' He pointed at the ground in front of him when Katherine arrived with a jug of ale and two horn beakers. 'I've laid out sticks to show the rough pattern of the rooms. I propose to have a plain roof and the front of the house will be simple, set with a door in the middle, and windows beside. From front to back runs a passage, and to the left of the door is the long, handsome room your father craves. On the right lie more rooms for family and servants, the kitchen quarters out at the back. What say you? Here, walk with me. I'll show you.'

He took her hand with a courtly grace and an impish smile as he led her through the 'doorway'.

'Here is Dickon's room,' he explained. 'Better start thinking of furniture and fripperies or your father will be disappointed. You do know this house is really for you?'

'Yes,' she admitted. 'Our family has been here many a year and he's set on keeping it that way.'

Hugh surveyed the land towards the river.

'I'll let you into a secret, Mistress Kat.' His black eyes sparkled at her. 'I brought some maps back from the priory yesterday, that show how the river silted up in times past and is now good, solid farmland. We'll reclaim more land and shore up the bank.'

'You've been exceeding busy,' she said. 'We'll be moving in on Friday at this rate.'

He grinned. 'I brought something else back with me, and this, too, must be our secret. I'd heard the new vicar was making changes, so I had a quiet word with the masons' foreman over there. He knew of a spare window and, as I'd set his wife's broken arm last year, he's grateful, so he offered to come over soon himself and set it in. The glass broke and the stone frame is cracked, but that we can make good.'

'For shame,' she teased. 'You're no better than a thieving magpie! Where do you think to put it, a great tall thing like that in our house?'

'At the back. But have no fear.' Hugh's eyes were merry. 'The window's small – from the side chapel. If it proves too tall, we'll make it fit, or make the walls higher. The front of your father's house shall be as modest as he asks, with nothing to make any king or lordling envious. But the back – ah, the back! The back of the house will be glorious – and secret!'

*

Dickon Wellman approved the plans and the former monk's change of occupation.

'They said you were a clever fellow,' he said; then, slowly, 'Now, this question of your name. Hugh has a good ring to it, but Beauchamp's a name that spells trouble.'

Hugh hesitated.

'My father was of noble stock,' he admitted, 'though I'll say no more. At fifteen, he alone of his father and brothers survived Bosworth.' His dark-browed face lit up in a wry grin. 'He fought on what I would call the right side, but many a more prudent man these days would say was very much the wrong one. Sir?'

For Dickon Wellman had made to speak, thumping the table with his fist.

'I say plain – if your father fought for King Richard, he fought on the right side, and I care not who hears me. Or at least,' there was a twinkle in his eyes, 'I do care, but you know what I mean.'

He fell silent for a moment, before saying solemnly, 'I'll tell you something I never told before. You'll not betray me. My old great-aunt told me this tale when I was a young lad. Said I should know, as the only child living.'

He settled his bulk comfortably and the young people listened intently.

'My grandfather, Ned Wellman, was the younger son, and back in King Richard's day he went off to fight for the king. Naught his parents could do and besides, he was in the right of it, they thought. Folk hereabouts felt the same, though to see the Blue Boar Inn nowadays you'd never know it. Aunt Margery told me the landlord near toppled off his ladder in his haste to paint over his inn sign and cover up the white boar that was the king's own emblem.

'No word of Ned reached the farm, but they heard about the battle and the king's death at the usurper's hands. Eight months after Bosworth Field, Ned Wellman reappeared, lean and angry, with money in his purse, and in tow a lanky boy who would be thirteen come August, Ned told them. He gave no explanation then or later, so the family put it about that he'd had a wife and the boy was hers, she having died. After a while, they scarce remembered aught different.

'Had he been at the battle, they asked in whispers. No, Ned told them bleakly. He'd ridden north the day before on the king's urgent business. He stayed tight-lipped about whether that business had prospered and he maintained a forbidding silence about the boy. One snippet he did let slip was that there had been an elder boy, ever an ailing lad, who sickened there in the north and died, and that the younger lad, Dick, almost followed him from the same fever. He'd regained his strength, but for some reason he lost his voice and had never spoken since.'

Katherine poured more ale for her father and the former monk. The farmer nodded his thanks and went on with his tale.

'Aunt Margery said people cast sideways glances at the boy. Dumb, was he? Simple more like, they said, but the family spoke out stoutly in his defence. 'Twas clear the lad understood every word and he did any task they set him. Right good at reading he was, writing and reckoning too. When Ned took on the farm, the silent boy became the grandson the old folks had always wanted, with his blue eyes and fair hair and the great height that I get from him myself.

'I say again, this must be secret.' His face was solemn again. 'My mother was the daughter of a Wellman cousin. Their marriage was a happy one, but I never heard my father speak but the once, on his deathbed. He gripped my hand at the last as he said something I've never forgot. A slow, rusty kind of whisper he had. "Dickon," said he. "When I die, go you and pluck a sprig of the green broom and pin it to my hat. Let me be buried with the flower of my family proudly worn."

'Well, I'll tell you! My thoughts whirled in my head, for I knew, as all men did in those days, what family it was that took their name from the *planta genista*, the green broom. He said, "Bosworth was our ending." That was all and he died an hour later, but I remembered my old aunt's tale and I did as he asked.'

Hugh cleared his throat, sounding loud in the silence that followed Dickon's rumbling speech.

'I ... I believe I take your meaning, Master Wellman,' he said quietly, and glanced at Katherine who was staring in awed silence. 'I'm honoured by your confidence and I will trust you too. When I was young, my father lost all, with naught but a few words out of place.' An unexpected smile brought out Hugh's dimples as he added, 'Mind you, those words were, "Henry Tudor has no claim to the throne of England" spoken out fierce and loud at Westminster. You can see the king's point.'

'Aye,' Dickon Wellman nodded sagely. 'See here, lad, I reckon we understand each other, so I suggest you take my name, there being no kinsman close enough to claim it. You carry on building my house and then help me with the farm. What say you?'

'Never mind what he says,' Katherine burst out. 'What of me, Pa? Am I invisible? Have I no say in this?'

'Foolish girl.' He stumbled to his feet, his cold anger more terrifying than bluster. 'Kat, when I die you'll be a woman alone and that's not safe, not nowadays. Not safe. I will have it so, for I see the hand of God. Here are you needing a husband and Hugh needing a home, so I'll see the pair of you wed before I die.'

*

The third dry summer in a row, this one was exceptional, and while Hugh and Dickon kept an eye on the levels in the well and dug out waterholes against drought, everyone on the farm and in the village set to with a will when they could spare the time. The master's new house was an object of wonder and soon enough the masons made such progress that the stone walls were at head height. To the delight of the old monks, Hugh designed a small alms building close by for them to live out their lives in comfort.

A day came when Hugh saw Katherine flushed and panting in the unfinished doorway.

'Pa's heard that a new king's man is due in town any day now. He's said to be Master Cromwell's man and has pledged to root out any who are not whole-hearted for the king.'

She jiggled impatiently as he took it in.

'I know I was angry about Pa's plan when he proposed it, but now …' She stumbled over the words. 'It is the only way to keep you safe.'

He opened his mouth.

'No, let me finish,' she said, scarlet but determined. 'If this man is full of zeal, he'll have lists of names and may come here seeking Brother Ambrosius or, worse, Hugh Beauchamp, son of a man who was loyal to the House of York. Let him find instead Master Dickon Wellman, a farmer who bought the priory lands fair and square from the king's appointed commissioner, and who is now building a fine, but not too fine, house with the aid of his daughter and her upstanding husband, a distant kinsman. And never a word of the silent stranger lad from the north.'

Their eyes met briefly, then they both looked awkwardly at the ground.

'I see,' Hugh said slowly. 'You may be right, Mistress Kat, but it must be done swiftly.'

'Pa reminded me that Brother Rohan was once ordained a priest, though most, including the old man himself, have forgotten. He sometimes married the pilgrims at the well, so Pa reckons Brother Rohan must marry us at once and Pa's friends in town will make sure it stands. He orders us to get home without delay and change into our good clothes.'

'Mistress Kat,' Hugh said gently, 'this is hasty and you should be courted, but I'll make you a good husband. This I promise.' The black eyes twinkled as he took her hand and chuckled. 'We'd better hurry. We must catch old Rohan while he's making sense, lest he marry your father to the donkey by mistake.'

*

'Lord save us, what a day!'

Dickon Wellman's bulk dominated his half-built room, with the space on the wall for his fine mantel and where the priory window would look out to the hills at the back of the house.

At mid-morning, the farmer had marched his daughter, her new husband, and the old monks to inspect the new house, and here he stood, arms akimbo, feet wide apart, with a sprig of broom in his hat. Although he had no idea of it, he looked remarkably akin to the King's Grace himself: a great height with the breadth running to fat, small shrewd blue eyes looking keenly out of a ruddy face, a sandy fringe of beard to match what remained of his greying hair.

'Here we are at last, my daughter and my son. Welcome to the family, Hugh. I'm proud to call you a Wellman. I trust you find yourselves well and truly wed this fine sunny morn?'

The bridegroom grinned as he nodded, and glanced fondly outside to where his wife was administering strong drink to old Rohan. The former monk, sitting on a log with his friends, was still, a day after the wedding, almost overcome by his brief return to old glories.

'Well and truly wed, Dickon, so you can stop nudging me. When are we to expect this zealous king's man?'

'Aye, well ...' Dickon Wellman's eyes almost disappeared as his face creased with mirth. 'Did I not tell you? Dear me, I must have clean forgot – what with all the jollity of the wedding feast. Word came after noon yesterday that 'twas all a mistake, and the new man was bound for Andover from Winchester with no plans to come here and interfere with innocent folk.' He gave his son-in-law a sly grin. 'Mark you, I saw no point in putting off the wedding.'

About the author

Nicola Slade is an award-winning, bestselling author of historical and contemporary mysteries and romantic fiction, all set in and around Winchester and Romsey in Hampshire – which is where she lives. *The House at Ladywell*, a contemporary romantic novel with historical echoes, won the Chatelaine Grand Prize for Romantic Fiction at the CIBA awards in April 2019 in Bellingham, USA. A follow-up novella, *Christmas at Ladywell*, will be published in November 2019.

Nicola is the author of the mid-Victorian Charlotte Richmond mysteries and the contemporary Harriet Quigley mysteries. *The Convalescent Corpse*, published November 2018, is the first in a new series, The Fyttleton Mysteries, set in 1918.

Website:	http://www.nicolaslade.com/
Blog:	https://nicolaslade.wordpress.com/
Amazon:	https://amzn.to/2o4PJ8C
Facebook:	https://www.facebook.com/nicolasladeuk/
Twitter:	https://twitter.com/nicolasladeuk
Goodreads:	https://www.goodreads.com/book/show/36237656-the-house-at-ladywell

Cerne Abbey, 1471

Rebecca Batley

'The king?' she asks. Her face is pale but perfectly composed.

'Alive. Back in London in the Tower.' A grim-faced Edward Beaufort speaks to his queen, and they exchange a look I do not pretend to understand.

My limbs feel like lead, like they will never move again. It has been scarcely two days since we landed on English shores and my heart, even more than my weary bones, aches.

We sit in Cerne Abbey,

Queen Margaret told me she admired the serenity of this place when brought here soon after her coronation, but I cannot see any beauty here. It is nothing compared with St Mary's in Warwick with its magnificent Beauchamp chapel, the resting place of my ancestors.

No one spares me a glance, and their voices continue to fly far above my head. I can hardly believe what I have heard.

How can this be?

I risk a peek at the men standing behind Somerset. Red of face and muddy, they have ridden hard to bring word, not to me, but to us, the great royal Lancastrian cause gathered here.

I almost want to laugh. We look like actors on a stage, everyone playing their part – the indomitable queen, prince, Somerset her loyal duke, John Courtney, Dorset, Exeter, John Morton and other rattled men – bit-part players all assembled in this small, draughty room.

How can we have come to this?

I am after all the Princess of Wales. The silver swan on my breast proclaims the fact.

'He will be coming for you.'

I turn my head to see that Somerset has the queen's hand pressed in his, his voice low and urgent. She stares at him so intently, anyone watching might think the look in her eyes is one of adoration. Indeed, it has been mistaken for such by those who seek to discredit us. But I know better.

This queen cares only for victory.

'Edward of York must seek now to press his advantage. Everything was in our favour, my queen, everything.'

They all nod their assent.

So why then did we lose? I want to shout.

Favour is of little use to dead men.

I know I should ask after my sister. Dear God – Isabel. They do not mention her. But then, why would they. . .

*

'. . . the body was taken to London. It will be displayed at St Paul's.'

They speak of the body of my father. The mighty Kingmaker. I wish I could say the news causes me pain, but I am too cold for pain.

'Such is the fate of all traitors,' Margaret snaps.

My husband stares straight ahead, impassive, and my chest hurts. It is so hard to breathe in this place.

'My lord, look to your wife!'

It is Dorset's voice, his lined face looming over mine.

I blink sharply. There is no need for their concern. I straighten. No daughter of Warwick will faint.

'Isabel?' I ask. My voice is quieter than I would like.

Dorset answers me.

'George once again turned traitor and is back in the confidence of his brother. Richard brokered a peace and it was together that the three sons of York rode out at Barnet.'

I almost smile at the mention of Richard's name. How he will have loved that! He told me as a child of the prophecy of York. The three suns that would burn so brightly they would obliterate the sky itself and shine nothing but light down upon England. He believed it so earnestly then, with the fervour of a devoted child. I'm certain he believes it now.

'I am sorry,' Dorset murmurs.

'Don't be.' My voice sounds strange to my own ears. 'What news of my mother?'

'Fled,' he answers, shortly. 'Your lady mother, upon hearing the news, took flight to Beaulieu Abbey'

*

I must be a bad daughter, for my thoughts immediately go, not to my mother, but to Elizabeth Woodville, so lately holed up in sanctuary herself, and forced there to bear her child alone. How I envy her now, for she will be safe, flying down the stairs into Edward's arms when he comes to her. Her hair will not be brushed and she will be dishevelled, but she will still be beautiful to him.

From persecuted wife of a traitor to queen again in one swoop.

*

The whole world has changed and I must change with it.

I am no longer a daughter of Warwick, only a princess of England.

I look to my husband.

'My lord, what shall I do?'

As one they turn. They had indeed forgotten I was there.

We have had so little time to speak, me and this husband of mine. It is only four months since he took me to wife on that freezing December day at the Chateau d'Amboise. It might have been far from Westminster, but it was a beautiful place, tall towered and glistening with frost. I had looked out of the magnificent vaulted windows and allowed myself to believe that my father would once again turn God's will in our favour, and make me Queen of England.

My husband is quiet and not unkind. He took me to bed as soon as word came from the Pope that it was right to do so. Our parents' fervent hope is that I will bear a son.

I search his face now for some compassion, but there is only exhaustion.

We are all exhausted.

'You shall ride with us – there may be a babe in your belly,' the queen announces, then turns away again, her great embroidered coat billowing around her skirts. I think, not for the first time, that she is born for this. A woman of action, embodying power. Her sharp movements thrust and parry.

In another life I had wished to be her. Only now I know better.

I also know that she is right. My course is late and, though there may be many causes for that, it is equally possible that I may be carrying a prince. There are no secrets here amongst us women.

'We must ride west, to meet Jasper Tudor in Wales. Recruit men along the way. By the time Edward has regrouped we shall be strong and ready to attack.'

Her hand cuts through the air like a sword and the men fall to their knees before her.

'God save the king.'

About the author

Rebecca Batley is an archaeologist, historian and writer. With a huge passion for history she is currently researching the life of Lionel of Antwerp.

Website:	https://thetravellinghistorianclub.wordpress.com/
Twitter:	https://twitter.com/TheTravellingH2
Instagram:	https://www.instagram.com/damagedbybooks/

The Corners of My Mind

Richard Tearle

'You never wished to be queen, did you my love?' Richard squeezed his wife's hand gently. 'Yet, 'twas I who made you one, though it was never my intention to do so. How could I have anticipated the events that led to it? Yet here we are: I, Richard, third of that name, the King of England and you … you, my Queen.'

Richard, perched on the edge of the large bed, stared at the ceiling of the small chamber. Beeswax candles were the only source of light, for the torch had long burned out and Richard had been of no mind to replace it. The moon, which should have been full and round, was dimmed red by the shadow of the night. A bad omen, men said, but of what they would make no comment.

'I loved you from the start, you know, Anne. Those childhood days at Middleham where we first met. I was thirteen, I recall it vividly. You nine, perhaps ten. As my brother George and I were put through our knightly training, you and Isabella would watch us, sitting on that low wall that was ever in danger of crumbling, laughing whenever we failed a tourney, clapping your hands with unashamed delight when we succeeded. You had such rosy cheeks then; your smile would spark the fire in them, I do swear! Such a pretty child you were, my dearest. Pretty and destined to grow into great beauty.'

Richard rose to his feet, crossed to the unshuttered window, fiddling nervously with the ring on his little finger as he gazed out over the cobbled courtyard one storey below

'I was devastated when Warwick fled and took you

with him.' He spoke to the eerily silent night. 'Devastated, yes. But that was nothing to the fury I felt when the news came that he had married you to Edward of Westminster. Never mind that your father had betrayed my brother – nay, all England, truth be told – by allying himself to Marguerite, the French she-wolf; he had betrayed *me*. It had always been understood that we would be wed, just as George was to Isabella. No one escaped my anger. Even Edward, my brother, avoided me though he still sought my counsel. And, as I have, with great shame, confessed to you, my dearest Anne, I found solace elsewhere.'

Richard bit his lower lip, quelling the tears that threatened behind his eyes. He took a deep breath, holding it until it escaped as slowly as it had been drawn. He winced as the uncomfortable pull of hardened muscle aggravated his blighted shoulder. Then he shrugged.

'I was young. Rejected – or so I felt.'

He turned his back on the bleak night, but did not close the shutters.

'You understood that, Anne, when I finally plucked up the courage to tell you. Yet you afforded nothing but kindness to John and Katherine, my bastards, when you at last made their acquaintance. How relieved I was that you accepted them. They, too, were grateful. Kate in especial. You were more of a mother to her than her own.'

A draught of air caused him to shiver. The candles briefly flared, sending dancing shadows across the wall hangings.

Ensuring that he would not disturb her rest, Richard carefully resumed his place on the bed, taking hold once more of Anne's hand, stroking the back of it and tracing a finger along the lines of the dark blue veins that stood up from the thin skin above them.

Such pretty, delicate hands, he thought. So soft. So gentle. So loving.

'I always tried to do the right thing, Anne. You believe me, don't you? I was never meant to be king, was never schooled for it. I always thought it would be Father before Edward, but that was not to be. Instead it was Ned and then, maybe, we thought, to follow him, George. Poor George!' He snorted a brief, low guffaw and then was silent for a moment.

'I know how you disliked him, Anne, and I don't blame you for that, for I well concur with your reasons. But it was never easy for him. Always overshadowed by Ned. George resented it, but Ned was always my hero. George wanted too much too quickly. Had he had an ounce of patience, he would have been king today, not I. We had our differences, George and I, the most serious being his treatment of you, my dearest.'

Another deep, indrawn breath as he brushed his thumb delicately over the back of her hand.

'I admit to being furious at that. How close did I come to killing him there in his own house where I searched for you in vain? Very close, I tell you. Very close indeed. And again, when you were finally found. I had begun to despair, I tell you true. Imagine my relief when the news came to me!'

Richard carefully raised her hand, placed a tender kiss on the gold band that adorned her wedding finger, then released it from his grasp.

Her fingers were cold. With tenderness he tucked the fur coverlet around her.

'There, that will keep you warmer,' he said, with a smile. 'Yes, there were occasions when I could have killed George. Yet, when Ned ordered me to inform him of that royal decision of execution, I could not do it.'

He released his breath from puffed cheeks, shook his head at the unwelcome return of memories.

'We had the most ferocious argument that we had ever had, Ned and I. Ned would not be swayed and my cause was hopeless. And so I did it. I told my George that Ned, our brother, our king, had decreed he must die. You should have seen his face, Anne. Even you would have taken pity on him. I recall I put my arm around him, though he shrugged it off and accused me of colluding with Ned. I will never forget how white his face had turned. Surely no man should have to speak such words to his kinsman, his own brother?''

Richard buried his face in his hands, the memories a writhing viper striking at his brain. With thumb and forefinger, he pressed at the corner of his eyes, drew his grip down over his cheeks, his mouth and his chin, feeling the harsh rasp of new-grown beard-stubble on his skin.

'And ... and our son, our own-born Edward. Our dear, dear Edward. It hurts me still, Anne, as I know it does you. Mine enemies say that it was divine retribution, but Our Lord would not take such an action, I am sure. If it were I, or you, who had sinned, why would He take our child? My faith has never wavered despite everything. I believe that Edward was simply not strong enough to overcome the sicknesses that so frequently afflicted him. If that be God's will, then so be it. There was nothing either of us could do, Anne. You did so much to ease his pains. How much sleep did you lose, sitting by his bedside night after night? Whilst I was busy with affairs of the realm? Oh, but how I wish I could have taken your place, given you some respite from your trials. The day he was taken from us – 'twas the worst of my life. The very worst. It will remain with me forever – when we dined alone at Nottingham and the messenger came with the dire news.'

Richard bowed his head, suppressing a sob. *Too many sad times in my life, too many,* he thought. The deaths of his father and elder brother Edmund, of George and Ned. Followed all too swiftly by his own son, Edward. So cruel. So cruel!

Now only he was left. Richard. The last of the Plantagenet name. He sighed again.

He even regretted the deaths of his enemies. Richard Neville, Anne's father, the mighty Earl of Warwick, basely slain by common soldiers and strictly against Ned's orders – though no doubt, as king, Ned would have ordered Warwick's execution had he been captured alive.

Nor had old King Harry deserved to die. He had been harmless in himself, but while he lived, Marguerite would fight in his name. The poor man had barely known where he was when they had entered that cell in the Tower and extinguished his sad life. The memories trundling in like a parade of ghosts, he even felt sorry for the French woman.

Not Buckingham, though. No, never Buckingham. Richard instinctively clenched his fists in anger. How he had trusted him, raised him up, only to be repaid with betrayal and rebellion.

'There are many deaths on my conscience,' Richard murmured. 'Will Hastings, Thomas Vaughan, Richard Grey, Earl Rivers.' He paused, other names, other faces prodding for his attention. He ignored them, swept their invasive presence aside. He raised his voice. 'But not Buckingham. I have no regrets over his execution'

He sat, staring at one of the tapestries adorning the wall, not seeing a single image that was depicted upon it. Not noticing that a draft from somewhere was rippling it, making the silk features of men astride their horses, galloping through the woods in pursuit of a white stag, appear as if they really were moving.

'But they were necessary, Anne,' he whispered. 'Their deaths. There was no question that all of them were guilty of treason. 'Twas all I could do! I know you advised me not to bestow that ultimate sentence, but I had no choice, my dearest. No choice at all. You do see that, do you not?'

Richard rose again, trembled as another gust of wind found its way through the window cracks and shivered through the room.

'I should close the shutters,' he said. 'The physicians told me that the fresh air would aid you, but it grows too cold.'

Nevertheless, he made no move to do so. Merely stood staring into the night. Said,

'But I dwell on the dark side of my life, Anne. There were so many happy times. None happier than those days together at Middleham after our marriage. Those long rides on the moors. How free we were, how free we felt! Days of bliss indeed! And the sheer joy of our son after those years of trying.' Richard chuckled. 'Oh, we did try, Anne. We were both so desperate for a child of our own, Nevertheless I feared it would never happen, that we would not be so blessed. I know you suffered with the birth, I heard your cries from without. Lovell and I, we were in the chamber, outside, listening, praying. I paced the floor while Francis tried to calm me – most unsuccessfully, I do not hesitate to record – and then, then there was a silence and I was a-feared that something was wrong. But 'twas not so, for there was another cry; a different one from the others. The cry of a new-born babe! I have never told you this before, Anne, but Lovell and I, we danced! Yes! We embraced and we clutched our hands together and danced in wild circles all around that chamber, such was our joy.'

He smiled, moved his feet in a brief, jigged homage to the memory of that euphoric moment.

'In spite of my impatience, I waited until the door of the birthing chamber opened and I was allowed in. Seeing you there, Anne, so pale, the sweat on your cheeks and brow but holding our little Edward, I do not think I have ever loved life – or you, my dear – more. Our son, our legitimate son, and my heir. No man could have been prouder. You handed him to me, you recall? And I, I was reluctant to take him for he was so small, so fragile, even bundled up as he was. I was so afraid I might crush him or, worse, drop him! That was foolish and needless, of course, and I did take him and brushed his round, pink face with my finger. I was bursting with pride just then. I wanted to tell the world of my joy; let every man see *my* son, be that man a king or a peasant.'

Floorboards creaked as he paced the room. He stopped beside another colourful embroidery that hung on the wall. Christ ascending to Heaven.

'Such a wondrous depiction,' he murmured. 'It comes to us all, Anne. Death. Death followed by Judgement. You – you will be judged favourably, for I never knew of any act that you might have committed that would keep you from God's presence. But I? How will I be judged? As a man who did the best he could? Or as a man who committed foul deeds to achieve his ambitions?'

He turned away, faced the bed. Fiddled once again with his finger ring.

'I know what some men have said of me, but they are wrong. How will I be remembered, Anne? God knows the truth, but how will Man judge me? 'Tis not so much what a man does, my dearest, but how he is remembered – never mind the truths of his life.'

Richard sighed a deep, regretful sigh. 'But that is for contemplation at another time, another day, another month. Another year.'

He returned to the bed and once more took Anne's hand in his. Lost in his thoughts, he did not hear the door open, nor Lovell's footsteps. Not until he felt a hand on his shoulder did he look up at Francis Lovell's grim face.

'My lord,' Lovell said. Then, almost as a whisper, 'Richard. She has gone. It is over. Let the women enter and tend her, prepare her body for her meeting with God.'

Richard, the king, the most powerful man in the realm of all England looked, blank, at his friend. Said, after a moment, 'How am I to live without her, Francis? How?'

About the author

Richard Tearle was born in Muswell Hill, north London, many years ago. He began working for the Ever Ready Company where he met his future ex-wife, before moving to the

Performing Right Society, collecting royalties for composers and publishers of music. Living in Barnet for a while nurtured his interest in Richard III and history in general. He then spent some time on the Kent coast before moving back to Barnet and later to the Midlands.

Richard spent the last eighteen years of his working life collecting autographs for the government, retiring in 2013. He currently works for free at Helen Hollick's Discovering Diamonds Blogspot, reviewing historical fiction, and loves every minute of it.

He has four children and an equal number of grandchildren, is a lifelong fan of Tottenham Hotspur and during the first two weeks in July he puts the 'Do Not Disturb' sign up and locks himself away to watch Wimbledon.

This is Richard's first published story, but he has a number of works-in-progress on the go. He now lives in the three-spired cathedral city of Lichfield.

Website:	https://rtslipstream.blogspot.com/
	https://discoveringdiamonds.blogspot.com/
Facebook:	https://www.facebook.com/richard.tearle.33
Twitter:	https://twitter.com/lordf34

Becoming White Surrey

Máire Martello

(For dramatic purposes, the date of Nicolas von Poppelau's visit to King Richard at Middleham has been changed from 1484 to the summer of 1485…)

The stallion emerged from the fog of the Yorkshire Dales. He stood still and erect in the outer bailey of Middleham Castle.

King Richard took a step forward and sharply drew in his breath. The horse was tall and snowy white, with the heavily muscled chest, thighs and legs of a workhorse. Yet his thick tail and mane swept the ground with the gentle grace of a lady's train and his fetlocks were covered in luxuriant feathers. His shapely brow was broad and intelligent, and the high curve of his neck was as strong as a Roman arch. The prominent, smoky eyes held a faint gleam of contempt and the nostrils breathed arrogance as well as soft vapour. He was a true destrier – the greatest of all the warhorses.

Dressed in black, with cloak, boots and velvet cap studded with seed pearls, the king reached out to touch the stallion. Startled, it spun back on its haunches, hooves pawing the air. The king's household rushed forward to protect him, but Richard didn't move.

Never had he seen a more majestic animal! And he was a man who knew his horses. His stables were full of coursers, rounceys and palfreys. There was Gray Gelding of Seville, Liard Clenvaux of Croft and Little White of Knaresborough.

'The stallion is a gift of Emperor Frederick,' said Count Nicolas von Poppelau in his clipped accent. He was on a diplomatic mission from Germany and had been granted an introduction to King Richard. 'He comes from Arabia. His name is White Syrie.'

White Syrie gave a snort of derision.

'I have no words to thank the emperor for such a magnificent gift,' said the king.

As the horse continued to paw the ground, the king's best friend, Viscount Francis Lovell, whispered into his ear:

'It's a fair horse, Dickon, but is very bad-tempered.'

The king smiled and said, 'No, Frank. He's mettlesome, but a most wondrous horse.'

Richard and Frank were young men. Frank, tall and blond, loved to laugh, while Richard was short, slim and serious. Frank was the chamberlain of the king's household.

'I assure you that White Syrie has been trained as a battle horse,' said Sir Nicolas hastily, 'and knows many of the fine manoeuvres of warfare.'

'It is a fine animal. Now we must see to your accommodations.'

'That is most kind. It has been a long journey. I've travelled from London to York.'

'I know the hardships of travel. I've just returned from Westminster.'

Richard took the arm of the older man and drew him across the courtyard to the inner bailey that housed castle and keep. Once the men entered the great hall, Richard turned to the count.

'There will be a banquet in your honour tonight. We have rooms for you in the western range. Shall you bathe before supper?'

'Oh, yes, Your Grace. That would be most kind.'

Richard turned to a dishevelled boy dressed in livery.

'Davey, would you please show Sir Nicolas to –'

Richard was interrupted by his very old retainer, Ralph Bygoff.

'Yore Grace! This boy canna look after such an important guest – 'e's bloody daft.'

Bygoff had long served in the royal household. Everyone was terrified of him for he was a man of strong temper. He was bent with age from years of travel with kings and like many old men was jealous of younger servants.

'Take Davey along with you. He can learn from you. Make sure there is plenty of dry wood and that a bath is arranged and candles are brought. Also, bring bread and wine.'

'Ah know what to do about winter livery, Yore Grace! Haven't Ah been doing it for more than sixty years for your mother and father and King Edward?'

'Yes, Ralph.'

'And Ah've been doin' it since *you* were a mewling babbie.'

Richard blushed furiously.

Unheeding, Bygoff turned on Davey and said with ferocity, 'Bring up Sir Nicolas's travellin' chests an' be quick about it!'

Davey fled to collect the count's chests. An uncomfortable silence descended only to be broken by von Poppelau.

'Oh!' He exclaimed. 'I almost forgot my letter of recommendation as well as letters concerning the Ottoman situation from the emperor.' He fumbled in his gown and retrieved several letters.

'I am happy to receive them. I will turn them over to my secretary, John Kendall. The council and I shall give them full attention.'

Bygoff brushed by the king and led the count towards his rooms. Richard turned swiftly round to Frank.

'Have you ever seen a more amazing horse? He is the finest war horse since Bucephalus!'

'Who's that?' asked Frank blankly.

'He was Alexander the Great's horse.'

'Oh. I was never too good at history.'

'Let's go and see him. He must stand sixteen hands.'

The two men ran down the stairs, their jewelled spurs sparking mightily against the stone. They crossed the bailey and barged through the mews and into the stables. In their haste, they sent dozens of chickens scattering.

There seemed to be a hundred stable hands and grooms at work, feeding and watering the horses, brushing them with curry combs, filling the feedbags with oats and horse bread, or hanging salt licks upon the walls. Others were sweeping out the stables or laying down peat. Horses were put out to pasture while others were brought in, their coats wet from the fog, hooves ringing brightly on the cobblestones. Goats ran about and Frank thought he saw a merlin, escaped from the mews, blundering about the low ceiling.

The men noticed that the king was among them. They solemnly bent their knees. Richard tried to regain his royal composure and bid them to go about their work. He called for the marshall of the stable.

'I'd like to see the white horse that was just brought in,' commanded the king.

'Aye, Yore Grace.'

Richard and Frank followed the man past twenty horseboxes until they came to the last.

'Has he been attended to?'

'Nay, Yore Grace. Ah sent young Titch 'ere to attend and 'e were near kicked to pieces.'

'Are you hurt, Titch?'

Titch, shocked that the king had spoken to him, replied, ''E broke ta handle of the feed bucket, Yore Grace. And 'e kicked my –'

Richard spoke softly to the horse.

'Why did you do that? Titch was only trying to help.'

White Syrie whickered ominously.

Richard again made an attempt to caress him. The horse reared up and charged the door. Richard held firm, but Frank shrank back.

'Perhaps he's demonstrating Sir Nicolas's "fine manoeuvres of warfare",' gasped Frank.

Enraged at being enclosed, the horse thundered about, his mane whipping madly, looking for ways of escape. Finding none, he butted his head against the sideboards and kicked frantically at the walls. Finally, he dropped his head despairingly. Richard watched him with sympathetic eyes.

'Just what I do when trapped in London,' mused Richard. 'We'll try again later.'

As they left, the marshall shook his head.

''E's a good 'orseman is Awl Dick but 'e'll not ride that one.'

The men walked back to the castle as the sun was sinking over the western range. They went up to the great hall and saw preparations for the evening's banquet going apace. The chief steward was ordering everyone about, shouting at the men who were hanging wall tapestries. Once they had been righted, he was over to the king's bench where Richard's canopy of estate was being hoisted on to rings in the wall. It was embroidered with the royal arms: two tusked white boars holding up the shield of England and York. Meanwhile, servants were pushing trestles against the walls and placing boards upon them, covered with fine linen. Torches were lit, the central hearth breathed fire and rushes sweetened with lavender were scattered over the floor. There was a delicious smell of roasting meats from the kitchens below.

'Come,' said Richard, 'let's go upstairs and change our clothes.'

They climbed up to the southwest tower. Frank noticed that the nursery door of Richard's son, Edward, was locked. Frank tarried, but Richard shook his head and turned away. The young prince had died a year ago.

As they entered the king's apartments, the groom of the chamber greeted them. A bath had been set up and Bygoff was testing the temperature of the water. He looked up at the young men and grimaced.

'Muckin' about in stable by the look of it,' he sneered. 'Modern royals! Know nothin' of the grand ole ways.'

A squire stripped the doublet and hose from Richard and drawing aside the curtain, he slipped into the scented water. Bygoff handed him a piece of Savoy soap and the curtain was discreetly drawn.

While the king soaped up, Frank perched carefully on a scissor chair that was one of the king's more unfortunate bequests.

'Have you heard of Henry Tudor lately?'

A deep groan was heard.

'Yes, he's apparently putting together a fleet to invade England this summer.'

'Just what we need – after almost two years of peace.'

'I suppose he's bored at the French king's court. I'm sure his dragon of a mother has persuaded him he's entitled to my crown.'

Tudor was the grandson of a Welsh soldier and exiled to France. Through the machinations of his mother, he believed he was the rightful heir to the throne.

Richard splashed around in the water, looking for his missing soap.

'Did you know that he has never fought a battle? Will you bring me my gown?'

Frank walked over to the stout four-poster bed that was heavily carved with Richard's white boar cognizance. He took the furred gown off the counterpane and handed it to the king.

'Now go over to my writing desk. You'll find a box inside.'

Frank obediently went to the desk. He opened it and there was a silver box. Within it was a red silk purse embroidered with two angels. It was a House unknown to him. Opening it, he took out a portrait of a lady.

'Who is she, Dickon?'

Frank started as Richard suddenly loomed up behind him.

'She's to be my new wife.'

'You must marry again and have more children.'

'So Parliament tells me every day. What do you think of her?'

Frank peered at the lady who was obviously of high birth.

'Who is she?'

'She is Joanna, the sister of the King of Portugal. She's a direct descendent of the Lancaster line which means our marriage will bring York and Lancaster together. But what do you *think* of her?'

Frank squinted at the portrait. She looked very sour.

'Well,' said Frank diplomatically, 'she has a nice complexion – no spots.'

'Aww, she's nowt but a right awl cow!' drawled Richard in his soldier's voice.

Both men laughed helplessly.

'Yet such a marriage would put an end to thirty years of war.'

Frank nodded. After a moment, Richard said, 'Now go to your rooms and dress. Don't forget to attend Vespers with me. I didn't see you there last night.'

In the moment that followed, the king went over to his night table and opened a drawer. He took out a miniature of his dead wife, Anne. He mused sadly on it before quietly returning it to the drawer.

*

That night, the king sat at the high dais with Rob Percy and Frank on his left and Sir Nicolas on his right. Other friends to join him included Sir Richard Ratcliffe, John Howard, Duke of Norfolk and Sir Robert Brackenbury. Sir William Catesby, John Kendall and various knights were placed at a lower table. The great hall was packed with nobles, clergymen and gentry listening to Sir Nicolas's Latin oration. It was greeted with enthusiasm, although the king would rather have listened to it in English – if he had to at all.

Richard wore a gold robe with slashed sleeves that revealed the crimson doublet underneath. Across his shoulders was a gold collar inlaid with priceless jewels. A black velvet cap was set upon his head at a rakish angle and sewn into it was the badge of York inlaid with marvellous pearls.

Once grace was observed, the guests washed their hands in the rose water provided for them. The trumpets announced the courses: salad with fresh herbs and imported vinegar and oil; meaty porridges and trout from the River Ure. Eel pies caused much laughter when Sir Nicolas requested some.

Frank intervened.

'Be careful, Sir Nicolas, not to over indulge. Remember what happened to our first King Henry.'

Sir Nicolas put his knife down gingerly. 'What happened to King Henry?'

'Lord Lovell is teasing you,' said the king in his quiet voice. 'King Henry is rumoured to have died from "eating a surfeit of eels". I believe it is nothing but an old wives' tale.'

To prove it, the king speared some and took a hearty bite. Everyone laughed and joined in.

Next came a huge beef roast with a rich pudding as plump as a sultan's pillow. A fat capon followed stuffed with truffles, oysters and chestnuts till it had grown to twice its size. The guests waited impatiently for the carvers to heap their plates while downing the Burgundian wine served up by harried butlers.

Sir Nicolas noticed that while the king was animated in his conversation, he barely touched his food and drink. Richard asked many questions about the German emperor which Sir Nicolas answered as best he could.

As the feast wore on, voices became louder with the wine and faces grew red with heat and excitement. Timid smiles turned to braying laughter as merrymakers forgot the slight but formidable sovereign seated at the high dais.

Then a blast of trumpets sounded and the great hall hushed in expectation. A marzipan eagle was carried in representing the German emperor's coat of arms. With its tongue and talons blazing bright red and its tail feathers spread wide, the eagle looked more like forged iron than a sweet designed by a master pastry chef. Sir Nicolas was overwhelmed. He turned to the king and cried,

'You are a man of great heart!'

Richard turned to Frank and eyed the gold collar worn over his robe. Impulsively, he removed it and dropped the jewellery carefully over Sir Nicolas's head. He then lifted his goblet to his guest.

'Your emperor is very kind to send such a great ambassador to my country. Thank him with all of my heart. Let us raise a cup to Emperor Frederick and his emissary, Count Nicolas von Poppelau. We thank him for his gifts today – especially our new horse, White Syrie.'

Goblets were lifted all across the great hall.

'Now let us repair to the gallery where my choir has set up.'

As the king said this, Ralph Bygoff approached. A frenzied whispering ensued that Richard attempted to quell with a dark mutter and a darker scowl. After an awkward moment, he turned to the assembled guests and cleared his throat.

'Let us repair to the gallery *within the hour.* This will give us time to honour our esteemed guest.'

Suppressed laughter ran through the hall, but the king said nothing.

*

It was long after midnight when the king and his friends returned to his chambers. It had been a splendid feast!

Frank grumbled amiably about his missing collar.

'Why, you yourself, Dickon, offered me one hundred marks for it.'

'I will find you something suitable to take its place. That is, if I'm allowed to untie the Privy Purse.'

'I will speak to John Hopton at the earliest convenience,' said John Kendall.

'By the way,' asked Frank, 'what happened in the gallery tonight?'

'There was a fist-fight among the choristers, resulting in broken heads and torn surplices.'

Grins broke out in the room.

'I thought I saw a black eye on one of them,' laughed Dick Ratcliffe.

'I will not tolerate drunkenness among my household,' Richard growled.

John Howard turned the subject.

'Did you hear what Sir Robert Brackenbury said tonight?'

'No, it was impossible to hear anything with those trumpets blaring.'

'We were discussing the Ottoman wars and the slaughter of innocents.'

'Oh!' Richard said passionately, 'how I wish that my kingdom lay upon the Ottoman Empire. With my own faithful people alone I would drive away not only the Turks but all my enemies.'

'You shall!' cried Dick Ratcliffe. 'And the men of Yorkshire will follow you into battle.'

'I may even join you in the fray,' ventured Kendall.

'If you do,' the king replied, his eyes twinkling, 'I will make you a knight.'

He smiled broadly when he saw Kendall's eyes pop.

Frank turned to the king.

'Do you think we can count on Percy of Northumberland if it comes to war?'

Richard shook his head. 'I don't know. He resents my continuing interest in the north.'

Frank shrugged. 'He hoped to be appointed Lord of the North.'

'Never. It is my home. The only way this land will prosper is if I keep a close eye on it.'

'I don't see what Percy would gain from siding with Tudor,' said Frank. 'Under your brother King Edward, he had all his former titles restored to him. What more could he want?'

'They always want more,' said John Howard.

'Aye,' Richard laughed.

Dick Ratcliffe spoke up.

'Everyone knows that Henry Tudor is a skinflint. I can't see him loading up Percy with land and titles.'

'Percy thinks he can charm his way into Tudor's heart and then worm his way into his purse,' offered Howard.

'I'll follow with interest his search for Tudor's heart,' smiled Frank.

Richard anxiously twisted the ring on his thumb while pressing hospitality on his friends.

'Shall I offer you some wine or comfits? The mayor of York, Tom Wrangwysh, sent me some fine apples. No? Perhaps a game of chess or dice?'

'Not tonight, Dickon.' Frank yawned. 'Every time I play with you, I'm skint for a month.'

'How about you, Jock? A game of chess?'

'No, Your Grace,' said John Howard. 'I've had too much wine this evening and my wits are addled. Also, you must remember I'm a greybeard.'

'Nonsense. You are as young to me as when you first served my brother twenty years ago.'

The king led his guests to the door, then he realized he was quite alone. He had dismissed his servants earlier in the evening, and even the young page who slept on a pallet was nowhere to be found. He absentmindedly sat down on the scissor chair and jumped up with a mild oath.

Although he was tired in mind and body, he knew he would have trouble sleeping. He would be plagued by dreams of his dead family. Then another image entered his mind. It was of a white horse, its mane and tail pluming in the wind as it pounded across the summer pasture of Middleham, trampling the fragrant clover beneath its hooves. He imagined himself upon that horse, riding so hard that no trouble could catch him.

He went to his wardrobe, hastily discarding his finery on to the floor. He reached for a worn doublet, pulled at its lacings and grappled awkwardly with his boots. He took up his cloak and grabbed several apples, stuffing them in his pocket. He yanked open the door of his chamber. To his surprise, his young page, Robin, was asleep on the stone floor.

'Robin! Get up!'

Robin opened his mild blue eyes and stared for a moment at his king. Richard saw vague recognition flickering in the child's face and grinned at his confusion.

'Your Grace, I was late to attend you and didn't want to disturb –'

'Never mind that. Go into my rooms before the chamberlain finds you. Get me a fresh shirt and lay it out. After that, go to sleep or I will take a stick and bat your brains out.'

'Yes, Your Grace,' smiled the boy wanly.

Before he closed the door, he saw the child fumbling among his fallen clothes. The king sighed: I must tell the master of pages to do a better job training the pages.

As he descended the staircase of the keep, he saw that the torches were burning low. In his excitement to see White Syrie again, he grabbed one so forcefully that it sent hissing sparks flying. His sentinels reacted fiercely at the noise, before a shock of recognition set in. As they dropped to one knee, he held a gloved finger to his mouth. Down the icy outside staircase he went and when he reached the courtyard, he swept his cloak over his shoulders.

Opening the stable doors, he stood for a moment until his eyes adjusted to the gloom. He placed his torch into a bracket and walked to the horse's stall. As he approached, he noticed a figure standing there. It turned towards him and for a moment his heart leaped in his breast. There was something in the figure's cocked head and slight stature that brought to mind his dead son. Grasping a nearby lantern, he flashed it upon the figure – and saw nothing but a grubby boy.

'Titch, what are you doing?'

'I've watched the 'orse all night, Yore Grace. I know 'e must be 'ungry, but I'm afraid 'e'll kick me.'

'He's vexed by his long journey from Germany. I've brought him an apple.'

'Oh, 'e'll like that. Mind now, 'e don't bite you.'

The stallion was nosing quietly in his empty feedbag. Richard struggled to pull an apple out of his snug pocket.

'Well, here goes,' he said quietly, directing a sharp whistle to the horse. White Syrie's head jerked up, but he did not move. Richard removed a glove, took his dagger and, cutting up the apple, held it out. The horse did not respond, but returned to the feedbag.

'We'll try again tomorrow.'

Richard retraced his steps to the stable door.

'Yore Grace!' Titch shouted, 'I don't like that 'orse's name!'

The king turned back.

'Why not?'

'Well,' said Titch shyly, cocking his head, ''e's in England now and not in – I forget where Yore Grace said 'e was from – some nasty foreign place. I think 'e should have an English name.'

The king raised his eyebrows. 'Then what shall we call him?'

'I dunno,' Titch said, 'mebbe Dobbin or Neddy?'

'No, those are workhorse names,' laughed the king. He walked swiftly back to the stall and stared at the now dozing horse. 'I shall name him after one of the finest counties in the kingdom.'

'Where would tha' be?' inquired Titch.

'Not too far from London – but it is nothing like London. It has white chalk hills and great forests. It's almost as nice as Yorkshire – though not quite.'

He took a fresh apple and whispered to the sleepy horse, 'Try this apple. Think of it as a wee gift from your new country.'

At that, the horse pricked up his ears and stared at the king. He ambled reluctantly to the door of the box. Titch retreated fearfully, but the king caught him by the elbow. After much suspicious snuffling, the horse took a slice and nibbled, then he gobbled the rest of the apple with such relish that the king nearly lost his fingers and his rings.

The apple dispatched, Richard snatched up Titch and held him over the door of the stall.

'Give him a pat, Titch. Don't be afraid.'

Titch did as he was bid. Though dirty and covered in straw, he felt warm and soft to Richard, reminding him again of another boy.

'I will call you White Surrey,' said the king. 'And we bid you welcome to England.'

About the author

Máire Martello is a writer and theatre professional who currently lives in Montgomery, Alabama.

The Lady of the White Boar

Jennifer C. Wilson

And so, he is gone. My Richard. Betrayed. Defeated. Killed.

Everything we worked so hard for, everything we enjoyed in life, torn away.

He was brought back to Leicester just yesterday, or what was left of him was, over that wretched bridge, with a lack of dignity my servants refused to let me witness. It was not befitting a king – I heard the rumours from beyond the walls of my room, the shouting in the street. Shouting that is rapidly silenced.

The one serving girl I brought from Nottingham Castle, Mary, is standing outside my door this very moment. I imagine her part-protector, part-guard. She won't let me leave. I've already tried twice, rushing at the door when she brought in my meal, then knocking, feigning the need for a doctor. She and Daniel are having none of my lies. They know what I was trying to do.

I know it is too late. I know I can do nothing for him now. But to say goodbye – surely that is not too much to ask? I have loved this man for more than half my life. Been his lover for most of that time. I've given him two children. I have the right to see him out of this world.

King Richard III of England. Cut down in his prime. In our prime. Just as life was feeling more secure. Two years into his rule, rebellions suppressed, changes being made for the good of the country. And then... and then Tudor. He will be calling himself King Henry VII now, but he's nothing more than an upstart. An upstart who has stolen a future I was working quietly towards, in the background, all this time.

At least my servants are loyal, to both myself and Richard's memory. They have brought me pen and ink, and fresh paper, as I requested. And I am content that my letters, when I can write them, will reach their intended readers.

It is strange to feel, at this moment, torn – between gratitude that so few at court knew my true status, my closeness with the king, and frustration at being uncertain where to turn next. To most, I was no more than a loyal servant – the tale put out that I grew up with Queen Anne in childhood, close companions through life. A handful knew it was Richard who placed me in his wife's household, not Anne herself. Perhaps it's safer that way, now everything has been thrown into disarray.

I wish he was here now. There are so many things to consider, people to write to, things to arrange. Not his funeral, of course. I'll wager Henry Tudor has some cruel plan for him there. It's the more mundane things I need to worry about now. After more than ten years living in the finest castles and palaces in the land, where exactly does the mistress of a deposed king belong? Who will retrieve my property from Nottingham, Windsor, Westminster? Is it even mine? It may seem selfish to think of gowns and trinkets, but if I don't, my mind will drift to imagining that bridge, those injuries…

'You should have let me go,' I mutter to myself. Nothing then could have been so bad as I now picture it, any moment I'm not distracted by another task.

'You wouldn't have thanked me.' Mary's voice startles me. I hadn't realized she was in the room – or that I had spoken aloud.

'I need to say goodbye,' I plead with her. 'You wouldn't be so cruel if I had been his wife.'

'No, my lady. Then Tudor would have dealt with you himself.'

She is right. As far as I am aware, Tudor doesn't know about me – or if he does, he doesn't know I'm in

Leicester. Not that he'll be here long before heading to London, to steal my love's throne, his capital.

At the thought of London, I almost crumple again. Mary rushes to me.

'Is there any word of Katherine and John?'

I can hear the desperation in my voice.

She shakes her head.

My mind strays again. But to my children, this time – our children.

Katherine should be safe enough, out of reach in Pembroke, but John is closer to the heart of things, even in Calais. I doubt Tudor will allow him to keep his captaincy, but will he let him keep his head? Perhaps we were too greedy. Perhaps I was too greedy – allowing Richard to raise him so high. But then, this isn't how any of us saw our futures.

Prince Edward should have lived, Queen Anne should have recovered. There should have been the joy of a new baby, another 'sun of York' to keep everything as it was. No Lancaster, and certainly no Tudor. Our children – Richard's and mine – should have spent their futures comfortably, in country manor houses, raising grandchildren for us – returned to the glittering Plantagenet court when they were old enough, perhaps befriended Edward himself, ready to move into the next reign with ease.

Instead, I am here, in a hurriedly rebadged inn, praying that if any in Richard's army do give me away, Tudor will see me as unimportant, not worthy of his attention.

He will have other things to occupy his thoughts, after all. His marriage for one. I wonder if word has reached Princess Elizabeth yet, or her scheming mother. The girl will be Queen of England soon, married to the man who has destroyed everything.

Perhaps, after John and Katherine, Elizabeth will be the third person I write to. With all our years at court together, and her sharp eyes and mind, I imagine she knows the truth. I've been waiting on her these past months and, to be frank, Richard and I were not always as discreet as we should have been, in the privacy of our own chambers. She might just welcome a friendly face, a companion by her side during the trials which are sure to lie ahead. My children are her cousins, just as Prince Edward was, whatever she may think of their birth. Perhaps she would welcome an ally in the royal household.

These are not plans I should have been making in these days.

Richard should have ridden back over that blasted bridge, triumphant, the last threat to his throne defeated, either dead or sent home in ruins, without the ability to return. Granted, I might not have been able, in my position, to formally greet him back into the city, but there are plenty who could have done. We would have reunited here, then dined in the finest rooms of the castle, before heading back to Nottingham, and on to London, aflame with glory.

I'm no fool. I know he would have had to marry again, to ensure an heir to the throne, and I know that it couldn't, in all truth, have ever been me. Rumours abounded of a foreign princess, a great alliance with the continent, but who knows what the future would have held?

Picking up the pen, I begin to write.

*

Hours later, the sound of a church bell wakes me. I've been slumped asleep at the small desk in my room. Aching now, I wish Mary had returned, forced me to leave my chair and sleep in the bed Richard brought with him. I haven't slept in it these past few nights, not since he left Leicester. Something stopped me. First, waiting for him, I suppose, and since – well, since the news, I haven't wanted to sleep alone in his bed. Ridiculous, really. There were many nights during our time together when we didn't share a bed, for plenty of reasons. But it's different this time, of course. I will speak to Daniel about moving from here tomorrow, to find somewhere new to rest my head. Whatever Tudor's plans are, for Richard and the country, I cannot remain here much longer.

For now, though, there is somewhere I need to be. Mary and Daniel must be asleep by now. Nobody can stay awake, watching, forever.

*

The street by the church where they've laid him out is oddly deserted, given a king is lying within. I suspect this is Tudor's work, trying to ensure enough people see the body to confirm that poor Richard is dead, but not so many that it appears he is mourned by the population at large.

The main doors are locked, but my luck holds. A side entrance has been left ajar, and nobody sees me slip inside. The place is cavernous, and eerily silent. Guards stand watch at the main entrance, but pay no heed to whether there are other ways in. Then I see him.

He isn't even in a coffin. Simply displayed on a trestle in the middle of the vast space. His wounds are on show for all to see. Somebody has cleaned him, at least, removed the blood – but I'll wager it wasn't done with love.

The pale moon has cast him in shadow, and the guards don't realize that anyone could approach him now, without their noticing. I take my chance, hurry across the floor, keeping my footsteps as light as I can, despite the weight of my grief, before a flood of relief when I have made it. Nobody else is here. Now, for a final few moments, he is all mine again – nobody in the world but the two of us.

There is so much I want to say to him, although I know he cannot hear me, but the risk of discovery forces me to remain silent.

'God willing, you can hear my thoughts just as easily as you would have heard my words,' I say to him, albeit in silence, going so far as to take his hand as I do. I'm shocked at how cold he feels. In a moment of folly, I almost call for a blanket to keep him warm, then remember it doesn't matter now, not any more. But nothing can stop me saying goodbye to him, no force in the kingdom would be strong enough for that. I don't wish to be here for whatever burial Tudor has planned, but I will take this moment.

And yet, the silence builds. What do you say to a man you've loved, and who has loved you, for years, but in an unofficial, almost illicit manner? Yes, there was entertainment in it, the secret life we built around ourselves – when he could retreat from court life, before and after he became king. But now it means I have no rights. I stood up for the rights and achievements of my children, but never for my own. I assumed, of course, that he would always be there.

A noise startles me back to the present. If I am to do this, I must do it now, and then go.

'Richard, know that I will not forget you, that I will do what I can to protect our children, and your name.' My throat swells with more tears, as I dare to say my final words to him out loud. 'I love you,' I whisper.

The sound that disturbed me before comes again, more insistent this time. I realize it is a quiet cough, a subtle signal, in the shadows.

'Mistress, you cannot be here.' Mary's voice hisses through the silence. We both look towards the door with fear.

I don't stop to think how she has found me. But, in truth, if I'm not in my room at the inn, where else would I be?

She hurries forward, her hand outstretched, clasping a letter. The seal has been broken, but it can't have been by the illiterate Mary. I don't waste my time wondering who might already have read it.

I glance at the open note, recognize the hand at once – Princess Elizabeth. She clearly decided to write to me more quickly than I decided to write to her. Whether a summons, an acceptance, a banishment, I have no clue, but I know I do not want Mary to witness my reaction, for fear that here, in this place, with Richard, my resolve to stay strong will fail.

I dismiss her, send her scuttling back into the shadows, and become aware that I haven't let go of Richard's hand. I don't want to. But I cannot read the letter properly without releasing him – and the return of the guards is still a risk.

Holding his hand against my chest, I lean forward, kiss his forehead in a gentle farewell, then replace his hand by his side. Allowing myself one final smile at the man I love, I open the letter fully, ready to face my future.

About the author

Jennifer C. Wilson writes historical fiction with spirit! Enrolling on an adult education workshop on her return to the north-east of England for work reignited her pastime of creative writing, and she has been filling notebooks ever since. In 2014, she won the Story Tyne short story competition, and has since been working on a number of projects, including co-hosting the North Tyneside Writers' Circle.

Jennifer's *Kindred Spirits* novels are published by Crooked Cat Books and her timeslip novella *The Last Plantagenet?* by Ocelot Press. 'The Lady of the White Boar' is taken from an ongoing novel, following the life of Richard III.

Jennifer lives in North Tyneside, and is very proud of her approximately 2-inch view of the North Sea.

Amazon:	https://www.amazon.co.uk/Jennifer-Wilson/e/B018UBP1ZO/
Website:	https://jennifercwilsonwriter.wordpress.com/

Facebook: https://www.facebook.com/jennifercwilsonwriter/
Twitter: https://twitter.com/inkjunkie1984
Instagram: https://www.instagram.com/jennifercwilsonwriter/

Richard Redux

Terri Beckett

He was bone weary, weary unto death. Every muscle, every fibre of his body ached, a symphony of pain that made his breath catch at every grace-note. He could not get a deep enough breath – his chest, constrained as it was by his cuirass, by breast- and backplate, struggled for air, and he was gasping like a landed fish. What air he did get was foul with the battlefield stench of burst bowels and spilt blood. Blood caked his gauntleted hands, his arms to the shoulder, clammy on his skin where it had seeped under metal and padded jupon, sticky and glistening on the bright steel of his armour. His surcoat with the royal arms was ripped and sodden.

'Dickon?' Francis' voice, hoarse. 'Dickon? Your Grace?'

He managed to croak an acknowledgement. 'Francis. White Surrey...?'

His beautiful destrier, pride of his stables, staunch battle-companion par excellence... So much carrion, now. Cut down in the final charge.

'Tudor,' he said. 'Francis, where is Tudor?'

'Someone look to the king!' Francis shouted over his shoulder. 'Dickon, you took a blow to the head. Tudor is dead. You killed him yourself.'

Someone was offering a flask – water? No, barley-spirit. He gestured it aside.

Tudor, dead? He found a brief jewel-clear memory – a white face, upturned, mouth gaping, eyes wide with terror. And the axe swinging down almost of its own volition to cut the man off from life and breath.

'Yes,' he said. 'It's over, then... *Deo gratias...*'

Someone – his squire? – was lifting the sallet helm from his head, and the mail coif settled around his shoulders. The arming cap had matted his hair into a sweaty felted mass. The air felt good. The fever-heat of the previous night had gone, sweated out, he guessed, by the exertion of battle. Francis had an arm around his shoulders, leading him through the carnage to his tent. He roused himself to issue the necessary orders, because that was what a king did.

'Tudor's body to the Greyfriars, for public viewing. Then he must be embalmed, to make him seemly before taking him to London. When we have the numbers of his surviving army, we will decide what is to be done. The Stanley brothers – I should never have trusted them. Francis, you were right. Do they live?'

'They do, Your Grace.' That was faithful Rob Brackenbury, going to one knee to salute his king.

'They are in your charge, Rob. The Tower, then trial for treason.'

Hands were stripping his arming jacket, his plate armour, leaving him in his sodden shirt and hose.

'Lady Margaret…' He thought briefly of her grief at the loss of husband and son, but also how she had repaid his generosity with the most heinous treachery. 'She is to be immured in a convent. Bermondsey, I think.'

'Dickon!' An objection from Francis.

'I do not make war on women.'

There was wine, and water, and fresh clothing.

'Now, I want a Mass of Thanksgiving as soon as possible. And send word to Sheriff Hutton. The children must be reassured. And, Francis –'

'Your Grace?'

'I want White Surrey buried fittingly. He was faithful and most valiant to the end.'

There were tears standing in Francis' eyes.

'I'll see to it, Sire.'

There was another message to be sent.

'And to the Duchess, *ma mere*. Tell her –' and he smiled, 'Tell her "Richard liveth yet."'

*

The road back to Leicester was crowded – carts for the wounded and the dead, and people gathering at the roadside for news of the battle. A ragged cheer began, gathering strength as they saw the white boar banner. 'God save King Richard!' and 'God be praised!'

Word ran ahead like rumour, and more folk crowded forward, waving their white boar bannerets, so that the herald, Blanc Sanglier, had to force a way through the press. The horse the king rode, unused to this kind of crush, was jibbing and dancing. Francis, riding close, used his own mount to control the crabbing sidewise gait. Richard, however, sat like a rock. He acknowledged the cheers, nodding to right and left – accepted a garland of white roses from a worshipful girl-child – but as soon as the door of the White Boar Inn closed behind him, he accepted the support of Francis' shoulder, and submitted to the ministration of Hobbes, the royal physician, and the surgeon in his train.

'What word of our losses, Francis?' He grimaced as the skilled fingers checked the bruises already purpling on his body, and leeches were applied.

'It can wait, Dickon, surely…'

'Now, Francis.' And it was the king who spoke.

'Richard Ratcliffe… Rob Percy, also. And your niece's husband, Lord Scrope –'

It was a rollcall of nobility, of the men who had ridden to battle with their king. And the commons, too, though names would come later.

'They will not be forgotten,' he vowed.

'You must rest, Your Grace,' Hobbes advised. 'You were fevered last night. The fever has left you, but its effects are still with you. Rest!'

It had the force of a command, and Richard knew better than to argue. Besides, he longed for the oblivion of sleep.

Hobbes and the surgeon left, after seeing the king to his bed. Once he had made certain that everything was in order, Francis also bade the king goodnight.

'God's peace, Your Grace. I'll be outside the door.'

'Thank you, Francis. I shall do very well. Get some sleep yourself. We have done ten men's work this day.'

'That we have, Dickon,' Francis agreed with a chuckle, and left him alone.

Richard lay back, carefully, against the heaped pillows of his travelling-bed, wincing as the battle injuries made themselves felt again. God be thanked, there was nothing that would not mend. The surgeon had left some pain-deadening potion, but he ignored it. The wine was good, and he cut it with water, the better to quench the thirst that still plagued him. The sickness, the feverish weakness that had plagued him the previous night, was eased. The light of the solitary candle Francis had left flickered on the walls, on the dark timbers with their vermilion vines – not for the simple inn of Leicester the luxuries of tapestry – and the silence rang in his head like a bell, echoing with the ghost-cries of battle.

Yes. He was remembering details now. The sickening instant when he became aware that the Stanleys had turned their coats again – the rage that surged through him, and the ice-cold realization that he must risk all now on one throw of the dice. *Alea iacta est.* Had he actually spoken that aloud? And valiant little Salazar, bloody from head to foot, clutching at his stirrup, entreating him to fly the field, to regroup and live to fight again. But no. *As God sees me, if I die, I will die like a king!*

He clapped his heels to White Surrey's sides, felt the power in the destrier's loins, bunching under him, the willingness for the charge, and they were flying down the flanks of the hill, he and the Household, arrow-straight for the knot of soldiers around the dragon banner. Smashed into them like a hammer-blow, mowing them down like grass under the scythe. The gigantic figure of Sir John Chenye loomed in front of him for just an instant before his axe found the man's life, then he swung the blade round to cut Brandon down, and the banner fell with him, and there – there – was the Tudor! A pale face, eyes stretched in terror, mouth gaping, and he struck…

'God forgive me,' he whispered and, ignoring the pain, struggled from the bed to kneel at the *prie-dieu* beneath the figure of the crucified Christ. He signed himself, bent his head on his folded hands. He murmured the *Te Deum*. '*In te Domine, speravi…*'

Tomorrow he would make confession, and hear Mass, and receive his Saviour. Until then, he must trust himself and all he loved to the hands of God. And surely he had been in God's hands this day, who had delivered him the victory.

*

The king spent three days in the town, recovering from his injuries – which, thanks be to God, were not serious. On the second morning, he went to where Tudor's body was displayed, as was the custom, and then to the church, where he ordered requiem masses to be said for all the dead.

He had Catesby compile lists of names. Those who had supported him, and died for it. And those who had supported Tudor, and survived. Rhys ap Thomas, who had taken oath that the invader would pass 'only over his body', and had broken that oath. John de Vere, Earl of Oxford. Reginald Bray. Jasper Tudor, the usurper's uncle, was reported killed. As was Edward Woodville. Of the others, he must decide who would be indicted for treason. The Stanleys, certainly. He had been too trusting.

But it went against the grain to be vindictive. He could consult with his advisers, and listen to them, this time, but those who sued for mercy would be heard. The French mercenaries would be shipped back to whichever gutter they came from...

*

London was London – stinking like a privy in the summer heat, raucous. They cheered him through the streets, their Good King Richard, and Parliament sent a deputation to congratulate him on his victory. Westminster Hall, where he met them, was heavy with the mingled reek of many sweating bodies. They called for his justice on the traitor Stanleys, and it was swiftly decided. Lord Thomas and Sir William would go to the block. Their families to be attainted. Their lands, titles and goods all forfeited to the crown.

'It is little enough,' Norfolk growled. 'Their treason could have cost you the crown, Your Grace.'

'God's mercy that it did not,' he agreed. 'We have lost too many loyal men... Master Secretary Kendall is to grant pensions to the families of those killed in my service.'

'Your Grace is generous.' The Speaker of the House cleared his throat. 'On another matter, Your Grace – I am constrained by your lords and loyal commons to beg your indulgence...' He cleared his throat again, shifting from foot to foot. 'On the subject of Your Grace's m-m-marriage...'

Richard closed his eyes briefly. The pain of that loss was still raw in his heart.

'What of it?' he said steadily. 'Name of God, my queen has been dead less than six months, and you would force another wife on me?'

The Speaker looked even more uncomfortable.

'My lord King, Your Grace, we mourn the loss of the gracious Queen Anne, of course we do, and the whole country shares in your sorrow, but...'

'I know, I know, I must needs have an heir of my body. Do you reassure my lords and commons that I am aware of this, and I thank them for their concern.' He got to his feet. 'You are dismissed.'

Outside, the August heat pressed down like a hot weight.

'Francis, I am for Berkhamsted. Will you ride with me?'

'With a good will, Your Grace!'

The country air was sweeter than the city stinks, and Richard felt his spirits rise. The sun was warm on his shoulders, and he pulled off his velvet cap to let the breeze cool his face and head, lifting also his hair from his neck.

'Francis, should I cut my hair? A shorter crop is the fashion now, is it not?'

'It is. As if you were ever a follower of fashion.' Francis gave his quirking grin. 'It is cooler, I can tell you.' His own mouse-fair hair was cropped short, and tended to stick up in spikes, like a hedgehog.

'I will give it consideration.' Richard smiled at his friend, and signalled his escort. 'Gentlemen –' And he urged his horse into a canter.

The Duchess's manor of Berkhamsted was a rich one, and in good order, as he would have expected, knowing his mother's insistence on overseeing her holdings. She had had the training of Anne, her daughter-in-law, and Anne had run Middleham with ease and grace. Anne... He could think of her now with less of the intense anguish of past months. It was half a year since she had left him.

He drew rein, letting his horse breathe; patted the sweaty neck, allowed the grooms to lead the animal away. His mother's steward hastened to bend the knee to him.

'My lord King...'

'Is the Duchess receiving, Michael? Announce me, if you will.'

She had been known as Proud Cis, and the Rose of Raby, and that legendary beauty was still evident in the fine bone structure of the face framed by the starched white wimple of a religious. She was in stark Benedictine black and white, but, as befitted her status as mother of the king, the stuffs were of the finest. The rosary in her hand was of ivory and gold, a gift, Richard knew, from his father after Edward's birth.

She rose from her chair as her steward announced him.

'My lord King…' she murmured, dropping into a deep curtsey, and then smiled up at him. 'My most dear son.'

'*Maman*.' He raised her, returning her smile. And kissed the cheek she offered him.

'Come, sit. Michael, some wine, if you would. Dickon, you look peaked.'

She sat down, arranging her skirts, and he took the stool at her knee as if he were not king but just the beloved last-born son.

'Are you well? There was some talk that you were taken sick.'

'Aye, before the battle. A fever, but mercifully brief. I had a battle to fight, sick or well, and the Tudor would not wait. You got my message?'

'Indeed. "Richard liveth yet." I have had masses said in thanksgiving ever since. I think I near wore out my knees praying for your victory.'

'God had me in His hands that day.' He signed himself automatically. 'Is it over now, do you think? This Cousins' War that has killed so many. My father, my brothers –'

'We must trust in God, my dear, that those lives were not spent in vain. Tell me. The Beaufort woman. You have not left her free to spread yet more of her poison?'

He grimaced.

'I was a fool, before. I was warned, but I thought to be merciful. No, my lady Scorpion is immured in Bermondsey Abbey, for her lifetime. With her son and husband both dead, she has no affinity left to call on. Oh, she'll be fairly treated – I make no war on women. But she'll not breathe free air again.'

'It is better than she deserves,' Cecily said grimly. 'And her son?'

'He will be buried as befits his blood, be sure. He was Richmond at one time, and a cousin.'

'Yes, you will do all rightly, that I know. And now,' she settled herself more firmly in her chair, her hands on the carved lions of the arm-rests, 'there is the matter of your marriage.'

He winced.

'*Ma mere*. Anne has not been gone a six-month...'

'I know, my son, and I know how dear she was to you. To all of us. Next month, on the sixteenth of September, you will hold her Month-Mind. But after that, you must think of another bride.' She fixed him with a gaze that held compassion and determination both. 'Is it the Portuguese match that you are considering?'

'It has the benefit of a double match, since Dom Manuel is desirous of taking the lady Elizabeth.'

'A good point. That would scotch those foolish rumours once and for all. But consider this, Richard. The Princess Joanna ... not young. Her chances of conceiving and bearing even one healthy child diminish as she ages. Sir Edward Brampton is well aware of this. He has made sure you are neither pledged nor promised. A younger bride would be better. The Infanta Isabella, of the House of Trastamara –'

'She is a child.'

'She is a woman, and of an age to wed, or her parents would not have considered it. Send a copy of your portrait to her. No,' she held up a hand to forestall his objections, 'it does not commit you to either one. The agreements are *de futura*. The succession is paramount, my dear. You wed for love once – as did I. Now you must wed for policy.'

He bowed his head, and after a moment, felt her hand on his hair in a caress.

'Dear son,' she murmured. 'God be thanked that of all my sons, he has left me the finest. Will you join me in my chapel to hear Mass?'

It was in a sombre mood that Richard rode back to London and the cares of his kingship. He knew that his mother the Duchess was right. She had never steered him wrong.

About the author

Terri Beckett is married, with one son, one grandson, and three cats, and, having lived in various parts of the UK and enjoyed four years in the Cayman Islands, is now settled in North Wales. She has been writing for some years, resulting in two published novels and several short stories in anthologies.

A lifelong supporter of the White Rose, and Richard III in particular, Terri had long wanted to explore what might have happened if Henry Tudor had not won at Bosworth. So, after retiring from more than twenty years of library work, she thought it was time to begin. The result is 'Richard Redux', published here, which is part of a full-length novel in progress. This alternative history will deal with Richard's relationships with Francis Lovell, his loyal friend, and with Richard's young Spanish bride. When it will be finished is anyone's guess!

Website: http://kymrukatz.co.uk
Facebook: https://www.facebook.com/terri.beckett.1

War of Words

Joanne R. Larner

'Come on, switch on the TV. You know you want to!'
Frank's hand reached for the remote control and brought the screen to life. He frowned as he realized he had done it unconsciously. He stared at the TV guide. Why had he put it on? There wasn't even anything on that he was remotely interested in. He scanned down the stations, then flipped to the recordings list.
'There! There! Stop on that one!'
His fingers paused and his eyes were drawn to one of the programmes. His wife, Alison, must have recorded it, as he certainly hadn't, but the title intrigued him so he pressed 'play'.
'Finally!'
He paused the playback and tilted his head, his brown eyes crinkling in puzzlement.
What was that? It had sounded like a voice, quiet yet distinct, but there was no one else up. Alison was in bed and he couldn't usually hear anything from the neighbours. Not at this time of night, at least. Why was he staying up so late anyway? He should really get to bed.
'No! No! You have to watch it, NOW!'
He had pressed 'play' again before he even consciously decided to do it. And then he became engrossed in the documentary.
'The King in the Car Park.' The story of the rediscovery of the mortal remains of King Richard III. It interested him because he enjoyed 'Time Team' and this seemed a similar type of thing. But he knew nothing at all of Richard III, although he had learned about the Tudors at school. And they were ruthless and cruel, especially Henry

VIII. He shuddered as he imagined being one of Henry's unfortunate victims. Apparently, this king, Richard III, had been even worse. He had murdered his young nephews to steal the throne, after having plotted for years to get it, and he had killed many more who stood in his way, because of his lust for power.

At least that was the Shakespearean version, according to the documentary. It was all news to Frank as, in his English class, he had only read 'Coriolanus', 'King Lear' and 'Macbeth'. However, recently there had been a change of tack. A group calling themselves 'Ricardians' reckoned Richard had been wrongly maligned all these years, that he was a good king: loyal, honest, just and courageous. Hmm. Intriguing… And the rather attractive woman behind the dig was so passionate about defending his reputation – she was even in tears at times. How strange! How could someone feel so strongly about a man who had been dead more than five hundred years?

He settled down to watch.
'*Good, he's hooked!*'

*

'Hi, love, I'm home! Look, I found a book you might like in the charity shop on my way home. What d'you think?'

Roy handed Sarah a thick paperback, obviously used, but in good condition. She took it with a smile; he was always so thoughtful.

'Thanks, Roy! I'll have a look at it when I've finished the one I'm on now.'

'*No, read it now, read it now!*'

They both paused. Roy glanced over his shoulder as if there was someone there, but of course there was no one. Sarah's fine brows were drawn together in a frown of puzzlement, but then she looked down at the book.

'*The Sunne in Splendour*. What's it about then?' Without waiting for his reply, she turned the book over to read the synopsis on the back. '"The magnificent, classic best-selling novel telling the story of Richard III,"' she read. 'Hmm, I don't know anything about him, but it looks quite interesting. Maybe I'll start it straight away…'

'*Yes! Another one bites the dust!*'

*

Alan sat in his cellar studio and strummed his guitar thoughtfully. He tutted as he heard the voice of Wanda, his wife:

'Alan, there's a documentary on you might like – "The King in the Car Park".'

He grunted. 'No, thanks. I'm busy writing a new song and I'm stuck. I need to concentrate.'

'*You really should see this, Alan!*'

Alan frowned, shook his head as if to get rid of an annoying fly and resumed his strumming.

'*ALAN! You can work on the song later. Go upstairs, now!*'

Alan swivelled to look over his shoulder, puzzled, but there was nothing to see. He turned back to his guitar, then felt a poke on his arm.

'Hey!' he shouted, putting down the guitar and standing up, before backing slowly to the stairs and running up them two at a time.

'I've changed my mind, Wanda. I've decided to watch it after all.'

'*At last!*'

*

Karen was in her caravan, but feeling a little afraid. There was a gale blowing outside, the wind whistling through the trees and buffeting the old caravan in sharp gusts, as if a giant fist were pounding the vehicle in anger. Surely it wouldn't be blown over, would it? Maybe she should take refuge in the local pub. But no, the pub would be closing soon and there had been no severe weather warnings. It would probably blow over soon. She would sit in the bunk with a nice cuppa and read her book of British history. That would take her mind off it.

Just as she began to relax and concentrate on the history book, she caught a subtle movement in the corner of her eye. She glanced up at the door. The book went flying as she sat up in alarm. A man was leaning against the wall, right there inside her caravan!

'Who are you?' she demanded, her eyes wide and her heart thumping as she stared at him. How had he got in when she had been so careful to lock up after she entered?

He was somehow incongruous, although quite handsome, with bright blue eyes and wavy, dark hair, which reached almost to his shoulders. He wore dark blue velvet leggings of some kind and a burgundy tunic with gold thread decorating the sleeves. A hat, like a cap or beret, was set at a jaunty angle on his head, with a jewelled brooch pinned on one side.

Strangely, she wasn't afraid, just startled.

He smiled, revealing a cheeky dimple, but said nothing. Instead he pointed to the history book, now lying open on the floor at a page with a large portrait. She looked at it and then back at the young man. Her eyes widened as she compared the two: the likeness was remarkable.

'But that's a medieval king – Richard III!' she stuttered.

He grinned again and bowed, sweeping his hat off in a courtly gesture.

'*You may call me "Richard", Karen!*'

'How do you know my name?'

'*I have been observing you for a while. I want to let you know that that book is wrong. I was not the man they describe therein.*'

'Oh!' she said, unable to utter anything more.

'*You must read about me elsewhere, think for yourself. Do not trust what the history books say.*'

'OK,' she said, uncertainty in her voice.

'Do you swear you will not believe all you read, without proper research?'

Something about him compelled her to nod.

'Good. Another recruit. I thank you, Karen.'

He smiled again and took her hand, brushing it with his lips as he faded, like smoke in the wind, leaving her hand cold. She shivered and picked up the book, running her finger over the picture of King Richard III. Her lips curved upwards in a grin and she realized that the wind had dropped.

*

The documentary was almost over and Frank sat there, intrigued, as the reconstructed face of Richard III was revealed. As the camera focused on the face, he realized he was holding his breath. The documentary ended and he flicked the controls to repeat the reveal. He paused the recording and stared at the face. A strange feeling coursed through him, almost physical – a wave of something that felt like recognition. He remained immobile, staring at the strong features, and knew that something important and transformational had happened.

He watched the whole documentary through again before he finally went to bed.

Alison stirred as he sank on to the bed, then she sat up and took a drink of water.

'You're late up,' she mumbled.

'Yes. I was watching that documentary you recorded for me.'

'What documentary?'

'"The King in the Car Park."'

She gave a sniff and then yawned.

'Wasn't me, babe!'

*

Sarah held the book to her chest. Tears coursed down her cheeks, as she felt a mixture of sadness, anger and frustration at the story – a fictional account, but obviously well-researched. But worse was the grief, a deep, aching pain that she couldn't explain – for a man she had never met, knew nothing about, who had died half a millennium ago. How odd but how powerful the feeling was. The pain still raw and tender at his cruel death and unfair betrayal as if it had only just happened. She knew she had to read more, that the last Plantagenet king had somehow wormed his way into her heart.

She picked up a pen and paper as the urge to write, unfelt for so many years, returned in a rush of inspiration. A poem was forming in her mind, almost faster than she could write it...

*

Alan finally put down his guitar and stood up, stretching out his back as he groaned at all the aches and pains. He shouldn't have sat there so long. Wanda had long since gone to bed and his dinner was most likely in the bin.

Then he gave a smile of satisfaction. He had written six songs. He had never been so productive in so short a time before. And what a new and original subject: King Richard III!

*

Karen was online, exploring the website of the Richard III Society. Excitement was growing inside her as she read about the last English king to die in battle. Somehow, she knew that this was the truth and that the traditional history books were wrong. When she read about his valiant death, fighting for his throne and his life against the usurper, Henry Tudor, tears pricked her eyes. He died 'in the thickest press of his enemies', surrounded by treachery and cowardice. So brave and so honourable. She had already learned about his just laws, his attempts to drive out corruption and his judgements in favour of whomever he thought was right, regardless of their rank, wealth or affinity. What a king England lost that day!

'*Thank you, kind lady!*'

She whirled round and saw the man himself, seated comfortably on her sofa, one foot resting on the other knee and a smile dimpling his cheek.

'Can you read my thoughts?' she asked, shocked – and wondering if he knew she was currently thinking how outrageously handsome he was.

He winked at her, his grin widening.

'*Do not fear. I will not intrude into your private thoughts, Karen. I simply wanted to know what you think about me, about my life. You are very receptive to vibrations from this dimension.*'

It was true. She had always been able to sense things that others could not.

'What do you want me to think?'

'*I want you to know the truth. I want you and others like you to tell my real story – use any talent you have to show me in my true light, not painted black with Tudor propaganda. They maligned my character with the power of words. I knew not that words could be stronger than the sword, yet they are. So, my new army must be wordsmiths, not soldiers; artists, not knights; musicians, not warriors. Thus will we lay siege to the towers of Tudor lies and bring them crashing down. And we have to win. This time the Tudors must be beaten – defeated by their own weapon.*'

He stood and inclined his head in a gesture of respect, before he vanished.

Karen already had an idea forming for a novel…

*

Frank laid out the paints neatly and placed the brushes in size order beside them. Gazing at the blank canvas, he pictured in his mind what he wanted to create: Richard's face, not creased with worry and grief, but young, vibrant and handsome, like the reconstruction. And his body, not twisted and deformed, but upright and normal, clad in shining armour...

As he made bold, confident strokes on the virgin white of the canvas, a figure appeared behind his shoulder, watching his efforts but unseen by him. Hours later, the shadowy form leaned forward to see as Frank painted his face, creating eyes that were almost alive, lips that looked like they were about to smile and hair that was glossy and thick, a dark, chocolate brown. As he finished the final stroke with a flourish and stepped back to assess his work, he felt a soft breath, like a sigh, just behind his left ear.

'*Thank you,*' Richard whispered. '*Thank you so much!*'

His army was growing stronger. An exultant joy leapt inside him as he realized the corrupt dynasty of death and deceit, the Tudors, would indeed be defeated this time.

'*Revenge at last!*' he breathed.

The Men and the Monument

Liz Orwin

Leicester Cathedral. The small hours of Friday 27 March 2015, shortly before King Richard's tomb is unveiled to the world.

The workman did not look up from his task, even when a tool crashed on to the tiles beside him. The contractor whose careless hand had been the cause snatched up the tool as if fearful the disturbance might unsettle a ghoulish presence. Fleeing with the offending drill, he abandoned his companion without a second thought.

The first man barely noticed, sweeping around the newly completed tomb with great care, even pausing once or twice to ensure a thorough job was done. When satisfied he could do no more, he swept the detritus into a dustpan.

As he left to dispose of the contents, two men stepped from the shadows. They sauntered around the monument, closely inspecting the plinth and the heavy Swaledale fossil stone resting upon it.

'Well?' said the dark-haired man, smartly attired in black. 'What do you think?'

'It's a little plain for my taste,' the taller man observed. He was strangely dressed, sporting a scruffy, brownish robe. 'Looks like the money ran out sooner than anticipated.'

A frown creasing his brow, the dark-haired man turned to his companion.

'So you'd have preferred something more garish?'

'Absolutely. Why bury a king and then apologize for it? If this is to be the mark of that man, let it be a great one. I don't consider this to be great.'

The dark man shrugged.

'I like it. Understated perhaps, but I know quality workmanship when I see it, and that counts for a great deal.'

'Not as much as appearances,' the taller man sneered. 'What's the point in achievement if you don't celebrate it?'

Paused opposite each other, they glared over the tomb, eyes locked as if in deadly combat. The impasse continued for some moments until the dark-haired man flashed a smile, his features handsome in the half-light.

'Perhaps you can't see this *is* a celebration, one with clean lines and minimalism instead of an ostentatious bronze effigy. Admittedly, it's a contemporary interpretation, but I consider it far more aesthetically pleasing than a gothic monstrosity over-compensating for something.'

The cathedral filled with silence as the tall man did his utmost to avoid responding. The dark-haired man snorted, as if unsurprised.

'The tombstone was cut from a quarry in Yorkshire. That's a nice touch.'

The taller man laughed. As his head snapped round, the pale, shoulder-length hair swung from side to side, lank and somewhat greasy.

'Hardly. It's simply paying lip-service to those who think the remains should have gone up north.'

The dark man opened his mouth, then seemed to think better of speaking and clamped his lips back together. This delighted the tall man, who grinned, revealing yellowing, uneven teeth.

'It's all so deliciously ironic. The king who was buried quietly and discreetly is now being argued over like the last goose at Christmas. He divided opinion in life – and still does so in death. How amusing.'

The dark-haired man turned, vanishing into the shadows. After another moment, his unhappy tone echoed through the dark.

'I don't consider it remotely amusing. All this arguing detracts from what's actually happening here. This stone, this event, and the tomb itself, are all a really big deal. Especially to me.'

The men stepped silently around the tomb, each mirroring the other's movements in a bizarre dance. Quite who was chasing and who was following was impossible to tell. When the taller man halted unexpectedly, his companion, almost directly opposite, stopped too. The men eyed each other once more, a silent weighing-up of souls.

As he spotted the brightly coloured royal coat of arms, the tall man rolled his eyes.

'This whole charade has rather surprised me. I never imagined a defeated and discredited foe would attract attention on such a grand scale. It defies belief.'

He sniffed and turned away, making himself comfortable on a lonely chair abandoned beside a pillar. Rummaging inside his robe, he drew out a battered old wallet and began sorting through its contents.

The dark-haired man walked around the tomb, and around again. Studying the pale stone, cut deep with a cross, he was lost in thought for several minutes.

'I say,' he said at last. 'Did you see the procession from Bosworth?'

The tall man barely glanced up from his wallet. 'What of it?'

'What did you think? Was it enough to commemorate a king, or was that also done on the cheap?'

The tall man smirked, transforming his expression into something rather sinister.

'This whole pantomime's being compared with the funeral of that lovely princess a few years ago. They're saying she got a bigger and far better show than an anointed king. But perhaps *she* deserved the recognition.'

'I've met her, y'know.' Steering their conversation, the dark-haired man watched carefully for a reaction.

'Really?'

'Yes, really. She did a lot of charitable works and we got talking.'

'Was she as pretty as they say?' As he leaped off his lonely chair, the tall man's face lit up like a child's. 'I recall her being a rather attractive blonde . . .'

'She has a certain charm, makes you feel like you're the only one in the room. We spoke for ages and she was unfailingly kind.'

'Lucky you.' The tall man's features resumed their careworn expression. 'The only woman nice to me is my mother.'

'That's because you're so serious, and suspicious of everyone's motives.' The dark-haired man gave a knowing smile. 'Not to mention your major trust issues.'

'So don't mention those trust issues, especially as you've plenty of your own.' The tall man gave a snort. 'And don't accuse me of being serious when you're as po-faced as any abbot.'

'I'll thank you not to knock my faith. It's a very personal thing.' The dark-haired man's lips thinned, as though he was struggling to keep control. 'Anyway, I didn't ask you here simply to trade insults.'

Huddled over, as he carefully studied the inside of the wallet, the tall man cast a small and pathetic figure.

'Well then, *Richard*, why exactly am I here? If you're finally going to forgive me, let's get it over with. I don't have all night.'

'Who said anything about forgiveness?' Richard whirled round and studied his companion for several moments. '*Henry*.'

Henry glowered. 'You invited me. What did you have to say if it wasn't to forgive the past?'

The dark man hesitated for a moment, then called him over. Together, they gazed upon the resting place of a king, once lost but now found.

Richard swept an arm over the tomb.

'Like it or not, you're a part of my history, and as strange as it might seem, I wanted to show you this.'

'To rub it in, you mean,' Henry snapped, recoiling at the honest response. 'I haven't come here to be made fun of.'

Richard stepped away from the furious Henry.

'You knew exactly where you were coming, so why the animosity? After all these years, I'd hoped your feelings towards me might have changed.'

'Nothing's changed!' Henry growled. 'I didn't care for you then and I certainly don't now. I only accepted the invitation so I could see what sort of circus this turned into.'

'But I thought we might at least agree a truce.' Richard frowned, confused by the unexpected hostility.

'I can't pretend to like you,' Henry said. 'And to do so before God would be a grave sin.'

Richard strode off round his tomb, talking as he walked.

'That I can accept. But as you seem intent on digging up the past, what's not so acceptable are your blatant double-standards. You took my life and my throne, my niece as well. Even your ghastly mother took my precious prayer book. And yet, after five centuries, you're *still* devoured by bitterness. By rights, it should be the other way around.'

But Henry had vanished, seeking refuge in the deep shadow around the cathedral walls. When it became clear he was not about to enlarge upon the festering grudge, Richard sighed and sat down on the plinth, fingering the letters along the side of the stone.

'The words they said today rang so true, Henry – you have no idea.'

Silence.

'*Grant me the carving of my name.*'

As Richard's deep tones echoed around the empty cathedral, Henry emerged from the shadows. His face was even more pinched and haggard than before.

'That was all I ever wanted,' Richard cried out. 'But you barely stirred yourself to do that much for me. When you finally did, it was only to soothe your conscience, not to properly honour a consecrated king.'

'I needed to ensure the throne was secure . . . there was so much to do,' Henry whined, fingering his tattered collar. 'Even your ghost took remarkable effort to defeat. All those rebellions and pretenders. It was exhausting.'

'You allowed my body to be defiled and denied me a king's burial. You took so much from me, but worst of all, you actively encouraged the despoiling of my reputation.' Richard's voice wavered as he spoke, the echoes wavering too. 'Throughout my life – and death – I have been guided by God, but even in this place of worship, it's hard to forgive your omissions.'

Gliding back to the tomb like a Halloween ghost, Henry halted behind Richard. He leaned in close, murmuring, 'Given the deep faith you profess to have, *Saint Richard*, I don't see how you won't forgive me eventually. If I was a betting man . . . '

Whirling around, Richard grasped a handful of Henry's robes and pulled him so close they were almost nose-to-nose.

'Whatever others think, Henry, I'm a man, not a saint. Indeed, I'm struggling to *ever* forgive you for that treacherous defeat. The Lord knows this. Why d'you think he's made me wait five hundred years? But when I learned the people had kept my memory alive by talking of me, writing of me, hating me, loving me, discussing me, and finally finding me, it was worth every moment. They even did what you couldn't – they *honoured* me the best way they knew how. It doesn't matter whether it was what we would have done, it doesn't matter whether that princess got a better send-off, it doesn't even matter that I'm staying in Leicester. It's enough – because I won't be forgotten again!'

'So it would seem.' Henry's tone was pure acid.

Richard drew a sharp breath.

'This indignation is rather misplaced. What can you say about your legacy? Your youngest granddaughter was more of a man than you or your sons.'

Henry's gaze dropped. Suspended in Richard's grasp, he seemed to just hang there like an old coat. Finally, he whimpered, 'I know.'

Dropping Henry so fast he almost fell over, Richard stared at the pathetic man before him.

'I insult you and you just take it. Why?'

'Because you're right.' Henry straightened his moth-eaten robe, then took a couple of steps away from the man and his precious monument. He did not look up at Richard, focusing instead on the royal coat of arms.

'My sons didn't live up to expectations. One simply didn't live, but as you also understand that terrible grief, we won't go there. The other . . . well, let's just say he's paying for his sins.'

'And so he should.' Richard made the sign of the cross. 'Amidst his utterly appalling actions, he systematically destroyed the rest of my line.'

'Not entirely,' Henry added, shooting a quick but careful glance at Richard. 'If he'd done the job properly, there'd be no one left to check that DNA-thingy with and you'd be just another box of bones in a museum storeroom.'

'Perhaps.' Richard's brow creased as he considered. 'But that means he missed another element too; his sister Margaret is a direct ancestor of the current queen.'

Henry's haggard face lit up. 'I didn't fail after all . . .'

'You mean the House of York didn't fail – despite the enthusiastic efforts of you and your tyrannical son.' Richard grinned. 'That's the point, you old fool. Elizabeth is the link, both in name and in blood. You did nothing, Henry, apart from take my crown and sire a child or two. The link is your *wife*. She's the route that connects us, and through which Her Majesty traces her ancestry. Don't claim credit where there is none. It's the Elizabeths of the world who should be acknowledged here.'

Henry said nothing, staring at a spot on the floor.

'And the current Elizabeth's done a great job, don't you think?' Richard expertly steered the conversation away from further conflict. 'The longest reigning monarch ever, a strong sense of duty, plenty of diplomacy, and heirs beyond counting. All sovereigns dream of that.'

'She's still had troubles to deal with.' Henry grimaced. 'It can't have been easy, given how the world's changed during her lifetime. I wouldn't have coped.'

His dark eyes watching Henry's face, Richard laughed.

'True. You're still firmly stuck in the fifteenth century. Just look at that dreadful old thing you're wearing. Do you *ever* spend money on clothes?'

After vanishing into the shadows, Richard had returned sporting a well-cut, bespoke black jacket. With auburn-tinted hair waving down to his collar, he looked every inch the modern metrosexual.

Henry glanced down. Noticing Richard's expensive, hand-stitched shoes, he scowled deeply.

Ignoring him, Richard concentrated on straightening his cuffs.

'This Queen's an example to all of us lot. I especially like how she's embraced an age of new technologies. She even has a Twitter account, giving "Sing a Song of Sixpence" an entirely new meaning.'

Henry's brow creased so much his little eyes almost disappeared.

'What's some stupid children's rhyme got to do with anything?'

'Would it interest you to know that rhyme's been associated with your family?' Richard chortled. 'I especially like one line: "The King is in his counting house, counting out his money." Who inspired that little number, I wonder?' Producing a smartphone from his jacket pocket, Richard thrust the glowing screen into Henry's face. 'See?'

Henry's face darkened as he pushed the arm away.

'It's just speculation, with no proof to support it. More importantly, there was nothing left to count in that treasury when I took over.'

'If I'd had a lot less treachery and a little more time . . . '

'Well, you *didn't!*' Henry yelled, his face suddenly diffused with heat. 'I defeated you and took the crown, so suck it up, Richie. I was king and you were dead. That's our history, like it or not.'

Richard dropped the phone into his pocket. 'And who have they been talking about for these past decades? Not you, Boyo. You just rock up at the end of proceedings and take the glory.'

'Yeah, and I took it from you fair and square! But now you seem to think the world owes you big time. It doesn't, King *Dick,* it doesn't owe you a dammed thing!'

Richard scowled at Henry.

'The fair-and-square bit might be open to discussion, but why are you so angry? That should be my role, all things considered.'

'I'm. Not. *Angry!*'

Visibly shaking, Henry took a deep breath and smoothed down the moth-eaten robe.

'I consider it all rather excessive . . . possibly the overreaction of a materialistic society lacking a deep-seated belief in anything. But mass hysteria doesn't even begin to cover the ravaging of a block of stone with a cheese-wire.'

When Richard failed to react, Henry gave a high-pitched laugh. 'That tomb's a joke. I wish I'd thought of it first, but then it'd be Wensleydale not Swaledale.'

Richard's voice was as calm as a summer morning.

'You'd never spend that much on cheese. Come to think of it, you'd never spend that much, full stop.'

'Whatever. It doesn't change a thing, Richard. I still won. I still took your crown, married your niece and am buried in the grandest piece of work a king could wish for.'

Richard gave a wry smile. 'But they don't talk about *you*, Henry. Not your pasty features, your funny eye revolving like something from a child's horror film, or those nasty little suspicions you constantly have. Even that incidental little society named for you – does it have thousands of members like mine? Have there been hundreds of books written about you? Were pictures of your discovery sent around the *entire* world? Did they line the streets to see *you*? No. You may have won the battle, Henry, but I've thrashed you in the popularity stakes.'

'I have a couple of pages on something called Facebook.' Henry's voice was very small. 'Or so I'm told.'

Footsteps sounded on the cathedral's tiles. The men stopped arguing and turned to look. An elderly lady in a floaty turquoise dress and hat to match walked towards them. Grim determination on her face and a patent leather handbag over her arm, she presented a formidable figure.

Richard stepped forward to speak, but she held up a gloved hand for silence.

'Gentlemen, please, this is hardly the place for raised voices and disagreements.' Leaning heavily on her stick, her bright eyes flicked from one man to the other, coming to rest upon Henry.

'Young man,' she chirped. 'I have several brothers and consider myself quite worldly, so I know the words you used have their best effect *outside* a church. Perhaps you should save them for a more appropriate occasion.'

'And who might you be to chastise kings so boldly?' Henry growled.

'The Duchess of York.'

As Henry snorted, the duchess gave him such a withering look, he froze on the spot. She smiled at Richard, who smiled back, enjoying Henry's discomfort.

Clearly well-acquainted with the visitor, he leaned over and whispered to Henry, 'This is another Elizabeth, and an exceptional queen consort. A little more respect wouldn't go amiss.'

Henry opened his mouth to speak to the duchess, but she had turned away. Fingering the pearls at her throat, she said to Richard, 'They're waiting, dear. Are you ready?'

Richard held out an arm for her to lean on and a smile creased her heavily powdered cheeks. 'Good lad. There's a gin somewhere with my name on it.'

'Where are you going?' Henry cried from the far side of the tomb. 'Don't leave me alone with this abomination!'

Untangling his arm, Richard turned to the duchess.

'Would you be gravely offended if I followed on?'

She smiled again, the blue eyes twinkling.

'Don't take too long or they'll start on the buffet without us.'

She melted into the shadows, the tip-tapping of her stick resonating through the cathedral long after she had vanished from sight. Richard walked over to Henry.

'I have to leave. They've organized a little get-together for me.'

'Who's "they"?'

'The Royals, past and present. They wanted to welcome me over, *officially* this time.'

Henry's face crumpled. 'You know some of the others?'

'Most of them.' As he caught Henry's expression, Richard had the grace to look away. 'That's how I met the princess. A few royals were waiting to greet me after Bosworth. My brother, of course, and another couple of Edwards. They were keen to acknowledge my bravery, which was most welcome after all that treachery. Then it just seemed to snowball, one royal after another. The princess came along about twenty years ago and we catch up quite often. She understands the raw deal too.'

Henry said nothing, his face a picture of misery.

Richard fiddled with a ring on his finger.

'I never asked. How was it after you passed over?'

'Deathly quiet,' said Henry, staring anywhere except at Richard. 'Only Arthur was waiting, and he didn't seem too happy about it. Elizabeth was nowhere to be seen, for reasons she's never fully explained. Since then, I always seem to be the one doing the meet and greet. Even my own mother, for Heaven's sake.'

'You're not alone there.' Richard was thoughtful for a moment. 'Have you met any of our predecessors?'

Henry shook his head.

'Not even your illustrious Lancastrian ancestors?' As the pale head still shook, Richard's eyebrow lifted. 'None of them?'

Henry's greasy locks swung freely. 'Not one. No Joans, none of the Henrys, no other Richards, not one Edward, and nary a single Elizabeth, apart from my wife. As you can imagine, that really grates.'

'You can meet them later, at the party.'

Henry scraped his foot along the length of the plinth. 'I'm not invited.'

Richard gave a low whistle. 'Are you sure?'

'You know full well I'm not,' Henry snapped, fiddling with a flower display at the side. 'Because you expressly told them so.'

'Ah, Henry.' Richard's voice was surprisingly kind. 'The ladies insisted on compiling the guest list and I suppose they thought you wouldn't want to come.'

'I'm busy anyway. Plans with Mother and Elizabeth.'

'But Lizzie's one of the organizers, she'll be there.' Richard shifted on the spot, his expensive shoes scuffing on the tiles. 'I'm surprised she didn't mention it.'

'Well, she didn't.' Henry's tone was as dark as night.

Richard considered. 'Well, one more won't matter. Come with me.'

'But Mother . . .' Henry squirmed, as though he'd been caught on a hook.

'I suppose you could bring her along,' Richard offered. 'If she promises to keep her condemnations to herself.'

'You know that won't work for any of us.' Henry began lumbering towards the door.

'Oh, give me strength . . .'

Dropping to his knees before the tomb, Richard clasped his hands in prayer, murmuring quietly in the darkness. When he opened his eyes, a white rose had been laid on the plinth before him, right beside the royal coat of arms.

'Henry!' he called into the shadows. When there was no response, he tried again. 'Come back, you old fool!'

'Why?' The voice was far away, deep in the dark of the night. 'This, as they say, is your party, and I've clearly outstayed my welcome.'

Richard picked up the rose and held it to his cheek. Then he leaned down and carefully laid the flower back on the tombstone.

'This has gone on long enough, Henry. Let's settle it once and for all.'

Footsteps sounded through the dark.

'And how might we do that?'

Hands clasped, Richard looked up into the eaves.

'I'll try to forgive all that you did, Henry. There's no guarantee I can but, as God is my witness, I will at least try.'

There was silence for a heartbeat, then Henry's voice echoed through the cathedral, his tone far lighter than before.

'That's very decent of you, Richard, considering. If it helps, I'll try not to be so resentful of the attention.'

'Thank you.' Richard broke off another bloom and put it in his buttonhole. 'And for the rose.'

Henry appeared beside him, studying the detail around the tomb.

'So much for a classy send-off. I couldn't find a red one anywhere . . . '

Richard gave a great guffaw and held out a hand to Henry.

'Pax?'

Henry hesitated just long enough for Richard to notice. He braced, but Richard didn't react, simply stretching his hand out a little further.

As Henry clasped the hand, he looked relieved. 'Pax. And for what it's worth, I think it's time too.'

'Good.' Richard shook Henry's hand with enthusiasm, sealing their clasp with his free hand. 'So, would you like to come to the party?'

'Really?' Henry's beady little eyes shone through the gloom.

'Really.' As they drifted into the shadows, Richard's voice floated on the night air. 'There'll be lots of people delighted to meet you. That charming princess too . . .'

The workman returned to his task. As he stumbled over the abandoned broom, his expression revealed an odd mixture of bewilderment and fear.

There, on top of the tomb, lay a single white rose.

He looked around in disbelief, as the faint sound of laughter echoed somewhere high up in the cathedral, along with the clink of glasses and buzz of a party in full swing. Then, as if a door had closed, all was silent.

Peace for the king at last.

About the author

Liz Orwin was born and raised in England, and has always loved history, especially the medieval period. After reading

Josephine Tey's masterpiece *The Daughter of Time*, she knew that Richard's world was where she wanted to focus. She joined the Richard III Society and has read avidly about the period for well over twenty years. After moving across the world to New Zealand with her family, Liz joined the branch of the Society there and is currently editor of its quarterly magazine.

Liz has been writing fiction for around ten years and has published numerous Ricardian short stories for the NZ Society, as well as two series of books set at the court of King Richard III. *The King's Niece* and *The King's Wife* (the Changes of Apparel series) concentrate on the young Elizabeth of York as she struggles to find her place at Richard's court during the traumatic months before Bosworth. *The Maid's Tale, Anne* is set earlier in Richard's life and is centred on the young Anne Neville, while the second book in this series, *The Maid's Tale, Johanne*, is a purely imaginary work, exploring what may have happened to Anne before her marriage to Richard, during those 'missing weeks' when she reputedly disappeared from the Duke of Clarence's household.

Liz is currently working on another tale from Richard's world, and is taking history papers when she has a moment of spare time.

Amazon:	https://www.amazon.co.uk/Liz-Orwin/e/B00CTFHX7W/
Facebook:	https://www.facebook.com/Liz-Orwin-717924464950846/

Eboracum

Kim Harding

City of Gates, streaming bright
blue of the Virgin in sky and fluttering fall
of ribbons entwined with mulberry
dark, rich wine-colour celebrating
this Crown of Days.

Great shouts banner across small streets
Breaking the balmy air with clamour,
With welcome, with joy;
Building a second wall, uplifting
spirit, state, worn Northern cares.

Blessings rise: Alcuin, Constantine, great St Peter,
cleansing the pall of faction, false friends,
old wounds of paper wreaths trailing...
my God-gift son rides through
arches unstained, unfathered, long wept.

I am no longer boy but man,
Bound by this fair city's grace
To deserve, to earn, to pray that
solar glory will round me as the rays that
dazzle and reflect, springing from God's own eye.

About the author

Kim Harding has lived in Yorkshire and County Durham for almost all her life. Married to the vicar of St Mary's Barnard

Castle (one of the Richard III Society's top five Ricardian churches), and with four now-adult (Ricardian-named!) children, she helps as a teaching assistant in the local primary school amongst other voluntary roles.

A Ricardian since her early teens, Kim is co-founder and Chair of the unaffiliated Northern Dales Richard III Group (NDRIIIG), which runs monthly meetings alongside a biennial study day attracting a variety of renowned speakers. With an academic background in Latin and English literature, as well as music and theology, Kim has written two (as yet unpublished) novels for older teens/adults in addition to writing and editing *Richard III's North*, a guidebook to Ricardian locations in the north of England published by the NDRIIIG.

Website: http://ndriiig.org.uk/index.php/richards-north/
Facebook: https://www.facebook.com/Northern-Dales-Richard-III-Group-1555111188072365/

Also available:

Grant Me the Carving of My Name

The original anthology of short fiction by authors inspired by King Richard III, also sold in support of Scoliosis Association UK (SAUK).

Praise on Amazon for *Grant Me the Carving of My Name*

'An inspired idea.'

'A mixture of the serious and the light-hearted, this anthology of Ricardian short stories is a must read.'

'A great compilation ... I love the idea that it is raising money for Scoliosis UK as well. A highly entertaining read.'

'Great book and brilliantly written.'

'What an enjoyable, entertaining, and (at times) heart-rending collection of short stories.'

'With a little something for everyone, this anthology delivers. I found the mix of genres very clever. Curl up with this book and enjoy a journey that will yield a rainbow of emotion and adventure. Well done to all the authors who contributed!'

Grant Me the Carving of My Name can be bought from Amazon via mybook.to/GrantMetheCarving or direct from Alex Marchant –
AlexMarchant84@gmail.com

Have you found a new favourite author within these pages?

Several of the authors featured in *Right Trusty and Well Beloved...* have written full-length novels about Richard III that you may also enjoy. Why not check them out?

Some examples:

Editor Alex Marchant ('If Only...') has published a sequence of books about King Richard III for younger readers (also enjoyed by adults) titled 'The Order of the White Boar'

Joanne R. Larner ('Grief') has also written the three-book series *Richard Liveth Yet* books

Jennifer C. Wilson ('The Lady of the White Boar') is author of *The Last Plantagenet?* and *The Raided Heart*, in both of which King Richard makes an appearance

Terri Beckett's 'Richard Redux' is taken from her Ricardian alternative-history novel *Shadows on the Sun*

Liz Orwin ('The Men and the Monument') has written two series set during King Richard's times: the *Changes of Apparel* books and *The Maid's Tale* books

Some of the authors have also contributed to two other anthologies raising funds for charities:

Yorkist Stories: A collection of short stories about the Wars of the Roses

Edited by Michèle Schindler

A collection of short stories about fascinating men and women who found themselves by birth, marriage, or fate on the Yorkist side of the Wars of the Roses. Richard, Duke of Gloucester muses about his brother, Edward IV; William Stanley contemplates marrying; Francis Lovell celebrates Easter; and others appear in a variety of situations in this collection. Even a ghost or two turn up.

Sold in support of Médecins Sans Frontières

The Road Not Travelled: Alternative Tales of the Wars of the Roses

Edited by Joanne R. Larner

Life is made up of choices and which road we choose to take may be a pivotal decision that affects our whole life and others' lives too. We often wonder 'What if...?' when we think about our past and about history. This collection of short stories from more than twenty talented authors explores some of the 'What ifs' associated with the Wars of the Roses. How would history have changed if one of the roads not travelled had been chosen instead?

The anthology explores some of these roads and includes most of the famous figures of the Wars of the Roses – Edward IV, Elizabeth Woodville, Warwick the Kingmaker, Anne Neville, George of Clarence, Francis Lovell and, of course, Richard III, to name just a few.

Sold in support of Scoliosis Association UK (SAUK)

All these books can be bought through Amazon, good bookshops or direct from the authors themselves (see individual author details). If you have enjoyed *Right Trusty and Well Beloved ...* or any of the other books, please consider reviewing it, to help other readers find and enjoy it. Thank you!

Printed in Great Britain
by Amazon